Pandora's Box

Pandora's Box

An Anthology of
Erotic Writing by Women

edited by
KERRI SHARP

Black Lace novels are sexual fantasies.
In real life, make sure you practise safe sex.

First published in 1996 by
Black Lace
332 Ladbroke Grove, London W10 5AH

Typeset by CentraCet Ltd, Cambridge
Printed and bound by Mackays of Chatham PLC

ISBN 0 352 33074 0

Contents

Introduction

*B*efore Black Lace hit the streets in July 1993, there was no imprint of erotic writing which was specifically aimed at women. As a gender, we have been told that we are not really interested in reading about sex unless it comes packaged as non-fiction in the pages of a popular magazine. A million Black Lace books sold is proof of how wrong this opinion was. Erotica for women is now seen as a genre in its own right and our success has prompted many others to follow the path of erotic publishing.

I feel privileged to have been part of something innovative; something which has given women a place to voice their fantasies. And those fantasies haven't always met the approval of the media. After reading extracts of the launch titles, a few newspaper journalists picked up on the fact that Black Lace books were unashamedly explicit. It seems they had been expecting romantic prose laced with a subtle hint of eroticism. Articles began to appear with shock headlines like *Women writers betray their own sex* and *Is this really the fantasy of British women?* Authors who were brave enough to be interviewed on TV and radio found themselves being accused of helping to destroy the moral fabric of British life and flying in the face of civilised values. An erotic writer was told on live television that she didn't deserve her sexuality. Things have improved over the past couple of years but it seems that we've still got a long way to go before we get to a sex-tolerant society which isn't riddled with double standards. Sexually explicit material still causes outrage whereas images of brutality and warfare are romanticised and accepted. As a species, we've been having sex for a long time. One would expect a little more tolerance and a little less hysteria over the fact that human beings have evolved with creative sexual imaginations.

Often, that which is dark and forbidden is most exciting – and many of our authors have explored this concept. Where Black Lace has succeeded is that it has given women a chance to indulge themselves in sexual fantasies which do not always conform to notions of respectability; a place where bad girls can have fun, too!

The Black Lace brand name has become synonymous with erotic writing for women. *Pandora's Box* is the first volume of extracts from the imprint. With 60 titles in print, I have every confidence that a second anthology will not be too far in the future. Thanks to everyone who has contributed to the series and put women's erotic writing on the map.

Kerri Sharp, February 1995

A Private Collection

Sarah Fisher

A Private Collection is Sarah Fisher's only Black Lace title. The story follows a young writer, Francesca Leeman, who is commissioned by fading society beauty, Alicia Moffat, to catalogue her very private collection of art. Alicia's inscrutable chauffeur introduces her to games of voyeurism and pleasure and Francesca finds a strange security in her new acquaintances' way of life.

A Private Collection

*I*t was almost midnight when Francesca finally, wearily, climbed the stairs to her rooms. She felt tired but exhilarated at the prospect of Catz's visit. During dinner she had seen him watching her, his eyes moving across her body, catching her eye; the cool sparkle of his interest had excited her. During dinner she had been absolutely convinced he would come to her room. Now as she opened the door she wasn't so certain. The wine and food had left her feeling relaxed and heady and she wondered if perhaps she had overestimated the strength of his desire.

She turned on the table lamp in the bedroom and slipped her evening dress down over her shoulders; beneath she was wearing a sleek black teddy and matching black stockings held up with a narrow band of elasticated lace. She rather liked the delicate sense of restriction they gave her. If Catz didn't come it was his loss, she thought, twirling around to admire herself. The reflection smiled back appreciatively – in her high patent shoes she looked wonderful.

'You look very beautiful this evening.' Catz's voice from the shadows of the bathroom made her jump. She swung around and in the light from the bedside lamp could make out the sharp pinpricks of light reflected in his eyes.

She backed away from the open door and swallowed. 'I didn't see you there,' she mumbled nervously, suddenly feeling a genuine tremor of fear. The fantasy of Catz's presence in her room and the reality of it were worlds apart.

He stepped out into the light. He was dressed casually in a white shirt – with sleeves rolled back – tucked loosely into a pair of jodhpurs. She swallowed hard; he was beautiful. His cold brutal eyes moved over her, lingering over her delicate curves, taking in the details of her undress. She shivered and stepped away from him.

'I thought you wanted me,' he purred softly.

Her mouth was dry, unable to find the words to answer him.

Catz shrugged and moved towards the door. 'Or was I wrong? Perhaps you prefer more tender meat these days?' He brushed slowly past her, the smell of him hypnotic, exciting – the tight swell of his muscles, the way he moved. Francesca turned and put her hand on his shoulder.

'Don't go,' she murmured. 'I want you to stay.'

The effect of her words was immediate. He swung round and encircled her neck with his hands, pulling her towards him. His hard lips sought out her mouth, his hot wet tongue forcing its way brutally between her half-closed lips. She gasped at the speed of his assault and at the same time let out a little desperate groan of excitement. This was all she had dreamed of; to feel him against her again, to feel his heat, to experience his strange, compelling eroticism.

His tongue sought out hers; she shivered and moved against him. His hand slipped on to her shoulders and his fingers slid beneath the shoestring straps of her teddy; she shuddered at his touch. He pulled back a little and looked into her eyes. She felt as if he could see every dark dream, every unspoken desire; she wanted to close her eyes against him but found it impossible. Part of her wanted him to share every secret sensation she had ever longed to experience.

Catz's fingers slipped out from under her shoulder-straps and down to the soft, smooth rounded lines of her buttocks. His hands rubbed the thin silk of her teddy against her sensitive skin and pulled her hips sharply towards him. She could feel the exhilarating brush of his hardening cock against her belly. His excitement thrilled her; she could feel her own excitement rising to match it and the beginning of the soft moist flow between her legs. She brought her hands round to cup his bulk but he pushed her hands away roughly, his eyes narrowing to thin dark slits.

His hands slid down over her thighs seeking out the fastening between her legs that held her undergarment closed. She knew she was wet and longed for him to free her sex, to push his cock deep inside her, to take her, to love her. Instinctively she thrust forward to meet his fingers; the snaps opened under his touch and she felt one cool exploratory finger run along the hot delicate fold of her outer lips. She gasped, pushing hard against his touch.

He pulled away, pushing up the fabric of the teddy so her sex was totally exposed. Gently he turned her towards the mirror so she could see herself. She gasped – the lips of the sex hung open, pink and moist, betraying their need for pleasure. Catz stood behind her and slipped her shoulder-straps down; his eyes held hers in the mirror, the soft fabric slithered down over the small orbs of her breasts. Not only did she feel the delicate caress of its fall but she watched in the reflection. Her nipples had darkened, gathering into tight excited peaks.

Catz's hands slid down to cup them, rolling their hardness between his fingers. The picture of her desire, framed in the mirror's shimmering silver, was electric. She could see the dark dilated pupils of her eyes flickering with a hungry flame of need; she could see the slight heady flush over her body. She whimpered and pushed her buttocks back against his thighs. In the mirror she saw Catz's sly smile as his fingers slid down to her sex, spreading the heavy outer lips, to expose the soft folds within; her clitoris, engorged and tender, pressed forward to try to meet his eager fingers. She stared into the mirror, watching Catz's fingers move over her, feeling the sensation, following the path of his caresses with her eyes; the combination was stunning in its intensity.

In the mirror, reflected like cold blue flames, Catz's eyes sparkled with desire – this wasn't an end to their game but just the beginning. His fingers slipped inside her and she felt her muscles close tightly around them. His thumb lifted to brush her clitoris. She moaned and watched the reddened lips of her reflection open breathlessly as, below, her gaping moist sex thrust forwards to draw his fingers further into her.

Slowly he withdrew his fingers and lifted the fragrant moisture to her nipples, drawing tight silver lines around them. From above she could smell the heavy musk of her excitement and again pushed back against the dark hard pressure of his erection. He resisted her though his lips now pressed against her shoulder, their wetness and the tight tiny caresses of his tongue making her shudder. She leant against him, drowning in the heat of his body against her naked flesh.

Slowly now his hands lifted and he guided her backwards; a part of her resisted, longing instead to watch herself, as her excitement grew, in front of the mirror. Catz sat down on the ottoman at the foot of the bed, his hands sliding down to her hips. She leant against him allowing him to guide her around until she stood beside him. His fingers brushed against her sex; she moaned and leant into his touch. He looked up at her, his eyes intense.

'Bend over,' he said coldly. 'Gerald tells me you've been a naughty girl.'

Part of her wanted to laugh at the game they were playing, but another part relished the idea of this poignant little punishment. She looked down at him, her eyes dark. 'The only thing that was naughty about it, Catz, was that you weren't there to share it,' she murmured throatily. Wordlessly he lifted his hand to the small of her back, guiding her forwards until she rested across his knees.

7

She resisted a little, afraid that she wouldn't be able to tell him she wanted this to continue if he asked her again. The hard muscles of his thighs pressed up against her belly and ribs. She felt heady and hot. Glancing up she could see them framed in the mirror: her, laying across his lap, breasts and buttocks exposed; above her, Catz's unreadable face staring back at her. The feelings of exposure and expectation were almost overwhelming; she choked back a little sob.

His fingers moved over her buttocks, softly stroking, seeking out the wet and expectant folds of her sex; she relaxed under his touch as one finger slipped into her. She eased herself back against him, opening willingly under his caresses. His finger slipped out and his hands moved away. She didn't move, her breath light and expectant . . .

In the reflection she saw his hand lift and for an instant was fascinated as it swung back in a broad arc. It seemed abstract, almost distant, and then she felt the white-hot sensation as his hand stung the soft cheeks of her bottom. The feelings snapped her mind back from the reflection to reality. She squealed out in surprise and pain, feeling the heat spread through her. His hand lifted again and she braced herself for the contact. The sensation was a heady mixture of pain and pleasure. Her bottom stung and tingled but between her legs the glow of excitement rose relentlessly. Now, with a rhythm established, he smacked her again and again. She moaned against his stinging touch, arching her back instinctively against the sensation of his hand, in doing so exposing her damp folds and tight dark bud.

She whimpered; his other hand slipped around to cup her breasts, his fingers seeking out the delicate sensitive buds of her nipples. He pressed and rubbed them, the tenderness a startling contrast to the smacking he was administering behind. Every smack sent a shudder of pleasure and pain through her; each time his hand touched her, her hips bucked while beneath her belly she could feel the hard and insistent press of his erection.

The combination made her frantic with desire. Finally, when she thought that he would never stop, he straightened his legs and she slithered unceremoniously on to the floor.

She crept up on to her knees, feeling a strange sense of exhilaration, and at the same time felt apprehensive at what Catz had planned for her. The cheeks of her bottom felt as if they were alight while between her legs a more intense inferno blazed brightly.

Catz looked at her impassively, his cold expression at odds with the excitement of his cock pressing against the tight fabric of his jodhpurs. 'Do you want more?' he asked softly. 'The choice is yours.'

Francesca nodded, feeling herself blush as the electric longing deep in her gut cried out for satisfaction.

Catz shook his head. 'You know that's not enough; I need to hear you say it. You have to ask, Francesca. You have to tell me you want what I can give you.'

Francesca felt her colour intensify. He was offering her a way out, a choice; there was never any compulsion. Wasn't that what Alicia had told her?

She looked up at him, her eyes bright with desire and excitement; she swallowed hard. 'I want you, Catz,' she said softly, letting her eyes travel over his muscular shoulders and down his suntanned arms.

'Look at me as you say it,' he said evenly.

She resisted him, looking down instead at the engorged, hardened outline of his cock forcing itself up against his belly.

His hand cupped her chin and purred. 'Look at me, Francesca. Tell me you want me.'

She looked into his eyes; they had an intimidating brilliance that unnerved her. He was temptation; he was desire.

Slowly but distinctly she whispered, 'I want you. I want everything you can give me.' As she spoke she knew that she meant it; she wanted him and his subtle dark understanding of her needs more than anything. 'I want you to touch me, I want you to teach me, I want everything . . .'

Catz nodded and trailed his fingers along the curve of her throat, his merest touch making her quiver as every nerve ending glowed white-hot. He drew a tantalising line up under her chin, skirting her lips, his eyes never leaving hers. She shuddered.

'Get on your hands and knees,' he said softly. 'On the ottoman so that we can see you.'

Francesca looked up at him and then silently complied. She knelt facing him, eyes bright, unable to disguise her eagerness. She felt excited at her unquestioning desire to obey him, to accept his every command.

Catz leant down and lightly pressed his mouth

to hers. His lips were wet and she opened her mouth willingly under the slow sensual enquiry of his tongue. One hand lifted to cup her breasts, his fingers circling her nipples; she whimpered at the gentleness of his caresses. He stepped away from her and slowly undid the buttons of his jodhpurs. She gasped as his hands moved lower, freeing the engorged reddened bulk of his cock. His other hand slipped something from his pocket.

She looked up at him, waiting, the sense of expectation growing with every second. He moved closer and let the moist tip of his erection brush across her lips. She lifted one hand to touch him; he moved back a little further, making her wait, making her longing so intense that she thought she might faint.

'Please, Catz,' she whispered. 'Please.'

He held her gaze, eyes mesmerising. She could feel a sprinkling of perspiration gathering on her top lip, could feel a deep trembling in the pit of her belly. In front of her, so close, he waited.

Gently he slipped a condom over the great curve of his cock and then, without hesitating, stepped forward. Desperate for him now, she grasped him to her and guided his shaft into her waiting mouth. The sensation made her shudder, the sleek engorged bulk of him filled her up. She closed her lips tightly around the end, sucking and teasing with her tongue, whilst her hands stroked back along the length of him, seeking out the tender delicate weight of his balls. As her fingers stroked down over them he shuddered and ran his hands over her neck, locking them in her hair before pulling her eager lips further on to him.

Behind them in the shadows the bedroom door opened silently.

Gerald Foxley had sat enrapt behind the mirror in the dark warm confines of the observation room, watching Catz's tender assault on Francesca's body. He had almost been able to smell the woman's excitement as Catz had encouraged her closer to her reflection. He'd wanted to reach out through the glass and slide his fingers into her enchanting dark depths as Catz had spread the lips of her sex. He could almost feel the scintillating bite of her muscles against the other man's exploring fingers. Her dark throbbing nipples had hypnotised him. He could imagine them hardening in his mouth, her body bucking and arching against him and the smacking; Gerald shuddered at the memory of it. The image of her swaying breasts, her hips lifted to receive her punishment. The way her belly had curved as she held herself ready in anticipation of the next blow. He swallowed hard, his mouth watering at the prospect of her compliant, submissive body.

Her willing submission to Catz had made him tremble. He'd relished the expression on her face – the ecstasy – as Catz had administered a sound spanking. She had practically begged him when he'd finished to continue, begged him to take her higher and further . . .

Gerald had watched mesmerised as Francesca had arranged herself on the ottoman for Catz's pleasure and gasped as she had guided his cock into her waiting mouth. As she began to suck at the other man Gerald could resist no longer. Seeing the way her belly had dropped instinctively to draw in Catz's phallus, Gerald slipped from his hiding-place and hurried across the landing.

As he opened the door he saw Francesca jump a little but Catz's hand moved across her body to steady her, stroking at her neck, teasing at her breasts. As he crossed the room Gerald slipped out of his evening clothes, his nervous fingers fumbling with the buttons and zip. In front of him he could see the curve of Catz's body as he contracted his firm buttocks, thrusting gently into Francesca's waiting mouth. Catz seemed almost oblivious to him as Francesca worked at his shaft.

He moved quietly around them. From the rear Francesca looked delectable; her hips had dropped a little to expose the soft inner lips of her sex framed by dark hair, and the tight bud of her forbidden closure seemed to contract rhythmically as she sucked Catz into her. Above the broad swell of her hips her body narrowed sharply before widening again at her shoulders. She looked beautiful – a classic erotic hourglass. Tangled amongst the soft tendrils of her dark hair Catz's hand twisted and moved as he encouraged her to explore him further.

Gerald speculatively ran his hands over her rounded thighs; she felt warm and deliciously slick under his fingers. For an instant he felt her freeze, her surprise and fear tangible and exhilarating. He leant closer to watch Catz stroke her, soothe her, petting her like a cat, and beneath his fingers Gerald watched entranced as Francesca began to relax.

He stepped closer to her; from the nest of gingery hair at his groin his slim cock jutted forward, and the very tip of it brushed the back of her thighs. Gerald shuddered excitedly and gritted his teeth. Francesca's instinctive reaction to his touch was to thrust back towards him, opening eagerly under his gaze.

He slipped one tentative finger into the swollen confines of her sex. The heat of it took his breath away; her muscles grasped at him, seeming to suck his finger deeper. He slipped another in and she moaned gratefully, the noise trickling from her mouth as it lapped around the bulk of Catz's member.

Catz glanced across at him, his eyes highlighted by icy glints of excitement, and he lifted a hand to Gerald's shoulders, his soft caress not quite hiding his strength. Gerald leant gratefully into his rugged masculine touch, savouring it against his cool pale skin. Catz's other hand moved away and he slipped a condom from his pocket. Gerald felt nonplussed and could feel the redness flush through his face. Catz smiled at him and unpeeled the packet.

Gerald swallowed hard, feeling uneasy and self-conscious as he moved closer to Catz, sidestepping the inviting scenario of Francesca's pulsating open body. With a gentle deft movement Catz unrolled the sheath along the length of Gerald's shaft. As he reached the soft junction where Gerald's erection met the delicate gathered swelling of his balls Catz ran a finger across the puckering. Gerald gasped at his caress, feeling the delicate skin tighten and ripple. Catz's fingers lifted again to Gerald's shoulder and with the gentlest of movements he guided the other man back behind Francesca.

Gerald was almost overcome with excitement.

He could feel the deep straining sensation building in the pit of his belly, feel the throb of the pulse in his throat. He was almost lost as he slid the smoothly covered curve of his shaft into Francesca's sex and was instantly rewarded by her grinding her buttocks hard backwards.

Enthusiastically he grabbed her hips, pulling her back sharply; her wetness enclosed him, sucking him into the moist sanctuary of her body. Under his fingers he felt her shudder, felt the tight grasp of her muscles around him as she began to move rhythmically back and forth against him. It was as if his mind travelled deep inside her, his every sense, every feeling, echoing through his cock before coursing into his feverish excited mind.

In front of him Catz had thrown his head back, relishing the eager attentions of Francesca's mouth and fingers. Gerald could see a silvery trickle of sweat forming in the pit of the other man's throat. Gerald plunged deeper as Francesca's sex seemed to open further under his thrusts. He pushed again and again into her, making her moan, her cries stifled by Catz's stiff excited phallus sucked deep into her mouth.

In front of him he heard Catz whimper; he glanced across to the mirror and knew all was lost. The triangle of straining and frenzied bodies, glowing and thrusting towards release, was captured inside the cool glass, giving Gerald a scintillating perspective. Francesca's breasts hung down, swaying in rhythm with Gerald's thrusts, her hips rose and fell against him. Crystals of perspiration along her spine glittered jewel-bright in the soft light from the lamps. Clinging around her belly were the damp gathered folds of her teddy, painting a startling contrast to her slick skin. Her neck was straining forward to take Catz deep into her mouth whilst one hand was lifted to caress him and cradle the heavy bulk of his balls.

Catz's reflection was arching back, hands kneading Francesca's shoulders as he pushed headlong towards his own climax. Behind Francesca, Gerald watched himself, his eyes bright, pupils dilated as he plunged his moist curving shaft again and again into the tremulous eager depths of Francesca's waiting sex.

Seeing the scenario unfold was too much for him. Gasping he looked away and felt the unstoppable white-hot contractions as the first of his seed spurted through him. Facing Gerald, still arched and desperately straining against Francesca's lips and fingers, Catz, unable to hold back any longer, bucked and called out as his own orgasm crashed over them all, the ecstasy of it contorting his face into a tight grimace. Gerald felt the last contractions of his own climax echoing those of his companion.

Exhausted, Gerald slid to the floor, trembling with excitement as above him Catz slipped from Francesca's mouth. Francesca rolled over, her slim body covered in the most delicate gloss of perspiration. She lay back on the bed, legs open, shaking violently. Gerald watched entranced as Catz moved towards her and knelt lovingly between her legs. Gently Catz pulled her shaking legs up over his shoulders. Francesca moaned as if to deny him as Catz plunged his tongue into her – the woman's hips thrust upwards to meet him. Gerald, unable to resist, clambered to his feet and eagerly watched the last delicious moments of their liaison as Catz skilfully brought Francesca to the point of orgasm. His fingers slipped inside her, where a few minutes earlier Gerald had buried his cock entirely, and his tongue sought out the hard swollen ridge of her clitoris. Under his ministrations Francesca moaned and whined with pleasure as Catz circled her hard engorged bud again and again. Her hips thrust up to meet his kisses, spreading herself wide to absorb every electric sensation. She gave herself to Catz totally, lifting her hands to hold her sex open for his tongue. Gerald watched hypnotised, seeing the intricate tracery of the man's skilled eager tongue against Francesca's body. Suddenly she let out a tiny intense shuddering cry and her body stiffened as Catz took her beyond the white-hot pulsing-point of ecstasy. Gerald, stunned by the display, sunk to his knees and sobbed with pleasure.

Elena's Conquest

Lisette Allen

Elena's Conquest was the first Black Lace book from Lisette Allen, who specialises in historical settings. Elena is a young Saxon girl who leads a peaceful life in a convent until one day in 1070, her village is besieged by Norman soldiers. She is captured by the dark and masterful Lord Aimery and taken to his castle where she discovers that her new master is captivatingly handsome and she will do anything to satisfy his savage desires.

Also available are *The Amulet* (set in Roman Britain), *Nicole's Revenge* (set at the time of the French Revolution) and *Ace of Hearts* (set in London at the time of the Prince Regent).

Elena's Conquest

*A*lone in his chamber, Aimery le Sabrenn, former penniless mercenary and now lord of Thoresfield, sat restlessly in his carved oak chair toying with his wine goblet.

Something was troubling him, and he knew what it was. He wanted the Saxon girl, badly.

He poured himself some more wine from the flagon, and drank it slowly. A single candle flickered smokily on the wall above his head. He stroked the tight scar on his cheek, which was hurting him more than usual.

The girl, Elena, filled his mind. He told himself that she was a rebel, no doubt responsible for the death of countless of his comrades in arms – a golden Saxon maid, to be enjoyed and cast aside, like the rest. Since his infatuation with Madelin – Madelin, who'd betrayed his brother – he'd humiliated many of them.

Madelin had made the mistake of thinking that

she still had some power over him, even after she'd betrayed himself and his brother to the Saxon rebels. When Aimery escaped from the rebels and tracked Madelin down at last, she'd pretended to be sorry about it all and actually welcomed him into her vile bed. She'd even cried over his terribly scarred face, because he used to be so handsome. Aimery had aroused her to her usual state of greedy lust, and then, when she was panting like a bitch on heat, he left her there, with just his bitter, ringing words of accusation for company. At least she still had her worthless life, though his brother Hugh had not been so lucky. The Saxons had tortured him, and castrated him, so that he was glad to die at last.

Aimery's hands tightened round the goblet, remembering. After Madelin, he'd fought the rebels so fiercely that even his own men feared him. And ever since that time, he and his mistress Isobel, had made a game of revenge, by selecting suitable young Saxon girls and making them plead for the pleasure he could bring them, before discarding them. Isobel always had plenty of ideas for their games – no doubt she had plans for Elena.

But, and Aimery frowned, there was something different about the convent girl. She might be one of the rebels, but even so he was strangely aware that he'd never encountered such beauty and innocence before. Soon, the innocence would be destroyed – they'd started on that process this evening. Soon she'd be as eager as any of them for sexual pleasure. She'd sidle up to him hopefully, as Isobel did, and when he grew tired of her she'd turn to other men for satisfaction, like the ever-willing Hamet or that young fool Pierre. Isobel thought Aimery didn't know about Pierre last night, but Aimery had spies everywhere. Since Madelin, he'd trusted no-one.

Aimery felt a sudden craving to know this girl in her innocence before she was changed for ever. He wanted to explore her sweetness for himself, with no-one else watching. He wanted to kiss those firm, sweet young breasts, and feel her yield to his thrusting manhood with all the passion he guessed she was capable of, until she was trembling at the very brink of ecstasy . . .

His mouth twisted mockingly at his fantasy. The little nun had cast a spell on him. All right, so he wanted to try her out. Nothing wrong with that. After all, she was his slave. Afterwards, he promised himself, he and Isobel would begin her training in full.

Elena had drifted into sleep, but it was a sleep tormented by her disturbed dreams. She was back in the bleak little dormitory of the convent; the cold moonlight shone in through the high, narrow window, casting its silvery gleam on the familiar flint walls and flagged floor. Wrapped in her coarse woollen blanket, she felt unbearably, achingly alone.

Then, still in her dream, someone gently touched her shoulder. She moaned and stirred in her sleep, and saw a wide-shouldered, tall figure standing over her little wooden bed, a man with a harsh face that was cruelly scarred. Aimery le Sabrenn. The shadowy horseman of her dreams. He was standing over her, slowly removing his clothes, and Elena cried out his name in soft disbelief. What was he doing here, in the convent? In her dream she felt no fear, only wonder, because she'd never seen anything so beautiful in her life.

In the smoky candlelight, his naked body was hard and strong, and marked by old sword scars that only accentuated the muscled smoothness of his skin. His hips were lean, his thighs heavily muscled, and his pulsing manhood was jerking upwards from that dark, mysterious cradle of soft curling hair, waiting for her, wanting her. With a soft cry of need, Elena reached out to him, and he was beside her on her small bed, cradling her to him, pushing back her long golden hair and closing her tear-stained eyes with his kisses. His cool, flat palms slid beneath her silk chemise to caress her small breasts; she moaned with soft delight and nuzzled against the smooth, muscled wall of his chest, a sweet, undefinable longing tugging painfully at the very pit of her stomach. Her dream had never been so clear, so sweet before. She never wanted to wake.

'Slowly, *caran*,' his voice came cool in her ear. 'We have all night remember? And you have so much to learn, little Elena, before the dawn . . .'

'*Caran*,' she repeated wonderingly. 'Please – what does it mean?'

He smiled softly, playing with her hair. 'In my own language, the language of Brittany, it means *beloved one*.'

Elena gazed wordlessly up at him, her eyes soft with desire. She reached out to touch the cruel scar that split his cheek, and felt the tense ridge of white skin against the tip of her finger.

The feel of it brought her to her senses. That face. That scar. *That voice.* Dear God, this was no dream!

With a cry of alarm, Elena wrenched herself back into reality. She was not in the convent, but in Aimery le Sabrenn's castle! And she was in the Breton's naked arms . . .

'No!' she cried out. 'No!'

But it was too late. Already, she was his prisoner. His hands continued their gentle stimulation, and he was still smiling at her. Her heart turned over. Heaven help her, but she *wanted* to be here like this! He had imprisoned her with some dark, potent magic, and she couldn't have torn herself away, even if she'd wanted to.

His erect manhood stirred heavily against her soft belly, sending strange, liquid sensations flooding through her helpless body. She let out a little, quivering moan and arched against him so that she could feel the rasping hardness of his long, muscular thighs against her own trembling legs. To lie in his arms, like this, to breathe in the warm masculine scent of him, was indescribable bliss. With a little shock, she realised that *this* was what she had always longed for, in her wistful daydreamings at the convent.

'You want me?' he whispered softly, his tongue flicking her earlobe, his hands slipping her chemise from her shoulders. 'You were dreaming of me? Tell me, *caran.*'

She shook her head helplessly, her blood already fevered. 'Yes, I was dreaming. I often dream.'

'You have the sight?'

'No!' How often had the nuns warned her not to

25

tell anybody about her strange premonitions? 'No . . . But this *must* be a dream.'

In answer she felt his skilful hand slide down to her private woman's place, where her flesh churned, soft and melting. 'No dream,' he said, 'but a reality. Elena, let me teach you.'

She caught her breath as he parted her moist lips and stroked, very gently with the pad of his thumb. He found her little bud of pleasure, and stroked it lightly so as not to over-stimulate her tender sex; Elena gasped aloud and went rigid, her eyes dark with sensation. 'Wh – what are you doing?'

His voice came softly out of the darkness. 'This, my little Saxon maid, is the heart of all your bodily delight, the tiny bud that flowers into sweet passion. You have never given pleasure to youself?'

She gasped again, because as his thumb stroked she felt the sweet, melting yearning spiralling like flames through her helpless body. She shuddered in his arms, realising that even if she had the choice she could not leave him now.

He bent his head to suck gently at the pink, tender tips of her breasts, and she writhed in rapture as the sensations poured through her. He raised his head to gaze at her. 'Your first lesson,' he went on softly, 'is to learn that it is not wicked, but wonderful, to pleasure one another so. As the lady Isobel pleasured you tonight. You enjoyed it, didn't you? The way her hot little tongue flicked at you – like this – and like this – '

Before Elena could speak, he had moved down the bed, and parted her unresisting thighs. Dear God. His head was lowering to her belly; she felt the hot warmth of his tongue at her navel, and then

26

it was sliding down her flat abdomen to slip between her lips and stab gently at that unbelievable pleasure place, just as Isobel had done earlier, only Aimery's moist, silken tongue was so firm, so fulfilling. She moaned, and writhed against his wonderful, rasping mouth.

He lifted his head to gaze at her, and his teeth gleamed whitely in the darkness as he smiled. 'You liked that, Saxon girl?'

Her body arched violently against him in reply, desperate for release. He could feel the waves of urgent desire spasming through her. 'Not yet, little one,' he murmered warningly. 'Not yet. You want to learn, do you not, about this wonderful instrument of pleasure?'

He reached to take her small, trembling hand and enfolded it round the throbbing shaft of his manhood.

Elena gasped aloud at the hot feel of it in her fingers. It was huge and velvety soft, beautiful to touch, yet so full of pulsing power. Would the lord Aimery do to her, now, what the terrifying Saracen had done to the lady Isobel? How could she ever take it within herself? Such a huge, swollen thing – almost like another limb – surely it was not natural! And yet she ached desperately to feel its silken caress inside her secret parts.

She snatched her hand away, trembling with confusion.

Aimery gave a low chuckle, and said, 'You will learn soon enough, *caran*, to worship my instrument of love. And, whether you realise it or not, you are more than ready to pay homage.'

His wonderful, teasing hands slid down once

more between her moist thighs. He ran a finger up and down her quivering flesh, caressing that wonderful point of pleasure with his circling thumb, until Elena was crying aloud with pleasure and thrusting her swollen breasts against the hard, muscular wall of his chest.

'Ready, little one?' he whispered. And he arched himself above her.

Elena stopped breathing when she felt the velvety smooth head of his penis stroking between her lips. There was no room for him! There couldn't be room! And yet, that swollen glans caressing her own engorged, melting entrance was a feeling so exquisite that she wanted it to go on for ever.

'Surrender to me,' he was whispering in her ear. 'Give in to me, Elena. Do you not desire me?'

'Oh, yes. Nothing more . . .'

With a husky groan of satisfaction, he thrust gently into her melting flesh.

And then, something happened. Elena felt the long shaft slip inside her, between her throbbing lips, and slide slowly up, into the very heart of her. There was a sudden, sharp pain that made her cry out, but the Breton kissed her mouth, and she forgot it in the wonder of feeling his manhood moving so slowly, so masterfully within her.

She lay back, breathless, her eyes wide open. He caressed her parted mouth with his skilful tongue, and then he began to thrust, gently.

It was the most wonderful thing Elena had ever known – beyond her dreams, even. Aimery was sending wave after wave of hypnotic pleasure flooding through her with each slow stroke. Once, he paused, and gazed down into her transparent, wide-eyed face; she gasped and clutched him to her, running her fingers up and down his muscular back. 'Don't stop,' she pleaded. 'Oh, please don't stop – '

For answer, he lowered his head to suckle at her aching breasts. Then she moaned with pleasure and instinctively coiled her slender legs round his thighs as he slid his hard length deep within her again. He continued to lick her breasts, sucking hard at the taut nipples, and Elena cried out with a new fever of delight as his hand moved down to touch her engorged clitoris, very gently. Her blood was on fire, her breath was coming in short, ragged gasps as wave after wave of rapture engulfed her dazed body.

'*Oh!*' She gave a long, shuddering cry and bucked wildly against him as her senses exploded in a shimmering orgasm of pleasure. 'Oh, dear sweet Christ . . .' He continued to move gently within her, his lips flickering at her jutting nipples, and she gripped his penis fiercely with her inner muscles, clenching at the wonderful, hard length of him with wild sensuality. She cried out, again and again, as he used all his skill to prolong her ecstasy. Then, as her strange little animal cries subsided, he lifted himself high above her, so that she could see the engorged shaft wet with her own juices in the darkness, and he plunged into her, over and over, driving himself to his own fierce, shuddering release. Elena quivered with renewed orgasm at the feel of his hot release within her. She held his sated body tight in her arms, glorying in the feel of his hard nakedness, her body still warm with delight.

Aimery was shaken as he lay there in the darkness. It was a long time, almost longer than he could remember, since he'd taken such pleasure in conventional lovemaking. She was truly innocent, just as she had claimed. Perhaps, too, her claim that she knew nothing at all about the Saxon rebels who visited the convent was true as well.

He reflected with some surprise that normally, a clinging, innocent girl such as this one would bore him out of his mind, and he'd turn away in disgust to find more sophisticated pleasures. Yet the Saxon girl's rapture had moved him strangely as he watched her exquisite face light up the darkness.

Not part of his plan, he reminded himself. His plan was to coldly arouse her, as he'd aroused others; to make her hunger desperately for him, then reject her. Remember Hugh's death – remember Madelin. Wasn't this girl tainted with the same Saxon blood?

He withdrew sharply from the girl's innocent, tender embrace and stood up. Elena looked up, bewildered, and saw how harsh his scarred face was in the shaft of moonlight that glanced through the shutter. She felt suddenly cold. 'My lord . . .'

Aimery reached for his clothes. He said, flatly, 'Not bad for a first time. But you still have a lot to learn. Isobel will teach you some new tricks.'

She shrank back as if he'd struck her. 'No! Not Isobel!' She put out one trembling hand. 'My lord – I only want you!'

Again, Aimery le Sabrenn felt that stupid wrench at the heart he knew he no longer possessed. He buckled his belt over his tunic and said abruptly, 'Isobel; Hamet; you will submit, Elena, to whoever I decide will teach you. Remember that you're nothing but a slave. You will do exactly as I say.'

The girl gazed up at him from the bed, her soft face dazed with misery. 'I am your slave, lord,' she whispered. 'I will do whatever you command. Only – will you come to my room again – like you did tonight?'

Aimery's mouth twisted as he glanced down at her. Her little breasts were adorable, her sweet face still flushed by that intense, fevered orgasm. Damn it, but if he stayed any longer he'd be making love to her again in a few moments.

'Perhaps,' he forced out coldly. 'But not for some time. As I said, you have much to learn.'

As her dark blue eyes clouded over in sudden pain, Aimery turned and swiftly left the room.

Elena lay on the cold little bed and hugged her aching body. She was racked with an empty sensation of loss at the memory of the sweet, dark pleasure the Breton lord had bestowed on her. Already, she yearned for him again.

She'd given herself, body and soul, to Aimery le Sabrenn, and she knew that she'd do anything, anything, to persuade him to return and pleasure her again in his powerful, exquisite way. And she knew, she was sure, that he desired her.

She had much to learn, she knew. But he was all that she wanted; and if this was to be a contest, then she resolved that she would win him.

Isobel, who had heard Aimery go to Elena's chamber and had suffered a violent hour of intense jealousy as the stupid girl gasped away her virginity, heard her lord return to his own room at last. Only one hour, and he had had enough of her.

Isobel cheered up immediately, and revised her

plans for tomorrow. Pierre would be a part of them, of course. But what else? With a sudden smile of pleasure, she remembered the little wooden chest where she kept her most precious possessions. She found the key and unlocked it, and fingered thoughtfully through its contents. At last, she withdrew a wonderfully carved piece of ivory that had once been brought to her by a traveller from the Mediterranean lands. It was shaped like a man's phallus, of more than generous proportions, and was designed, with careful carvings and protuberances, to stimulate a woman's pleasure zones; though not all women were capable of taking the huge shaft within themselves, especially not virginal Saxons. By the time Isobel and Pierre had finished with her, the girl wouldn't even *want* Aimery to touch her again for, oh, a good while.

Isobel fondled the instrument, rubbing it gently against her still tingling breasts until her nipples peaked and strained against the fabric of her shift. She smiled, imagining the Saxon slut's innocent face when confronted with this formidable weapon. Would Isobel show it to her first? Or would she wait for Pierre to finish with the girl, and then ...

Her green eyes gleaming with anticipation, Isobel kissed the ivory phallus and locked it away in its box. Then she went to bed, and laid her plans for tomorrow.

Early the next morning, Elena woke with a start. She sat up jerkily, feeling frightened and confused. Then the sounds of the castle courtyard came floating up through her narrow window, and she remembered. The early morning sunlight danced across her bed. Somewhere, a distant bell tolled.

The hour of prime. At the convent, the nuns would be filing into the little chapel for the first service.

No. The convent no longer existed. That life was over.

Elena slid from her rumpled bed, her skin golden in the sunlight, and ran her hands dreamily through her tousled blonde hair. Her naked flesh was warm and sensitive; her breasts softly flushed. Had last night really happened? Or was it all a dream? The colour rose in her cheeks as she remembered. Walking slowly to the window, she pushed the oiled hide shutter to one side and peeped out.

It was all true. She was really here, in the very heart of Aimery le Sabrenn's northern stronghold. The courtyard below was already a hive of early morning activity, full of bustle and noise. Servants from the kitchen were hurrying across to the bakehouse carrying trays of warm, scented bread; young squires frowned in concentration as they carefully polished their masters' armour on the trestles set up outside the guardhouse; a groom was leading a big warhorse from the stables, while some female serfs giggled and gossiped as they scattered grain to the hens.

Aimery's castle. Aimery's people. And last night, Aimery le Sabrenn had taken her in his arms . . .

Elena breathed in deeply, the sunshine warm on her face and her bare shoulders. This was to be her new life. There was no going back now. She knew that, and accepted it willingly. Her heart stirring in that knowledge, like a challenge, she turned to pick up her silk chemise from the floor, where the lord Aimery had cast it so carelessly last night. She held the soft fabric to her cheek.

Suddenly, the door opened. Elena looked up, startled, as the lady Isobel glided in; she looked exquisite in her beautiful green silk gown, with her dark hair coiled smoothly at the nape of her neck. Over her arm was a folded garment of rough homespun wool.

'My dear,' she purred, 'I trust that you slept well after our little *entertainment* last night?'

Elena, conscious of Isobel's slanting green eyes flickering with interest over her vulnerable, naked body, clasped the silk chemise she'd just picked up close to her breasts and said quietly, 'Thank you, my lady. I slept well.'

Isobel's words were kind enough, but there was something cold, assessing, in her eyes. Elena shivered suddenly, in spite of the warmth of the room.

Isobel's eyes rested on the beautiful silk chemise Elena was holding, and her mouth curled in amusement. 'As for today,' she went on briskly, 'I'm sure you understand, Elena, that as a serf you are expected to earn your keep. Edith, the housekeeper, is expecting you in the kitchens this morning. Here – I have brought you suitable clothing.' And she pressed a coarse serf's tunic into Elena's hands.

Elena's blue eys widened; she could not stop her gaze wandering to the beautiful gown she had worn the night before, lying on the oak chest at the foot of her bed. 'The – the kitchens?' she stammered out in confusion. 'But last night my lord Aimery said – '

Isobel's eyes snapped with annoyance, and she

arched her exquisitely shaped dark eyebrows. 'Oh, dear. I do hope you're not going to be difficult, Elena. Naturally, I am informing you of Lord Aimery's specific commands, however could you think otherwise?'

Elena swallowed down the sudden ache in her throat. Last night she'd been too eager, too open. She'd repelled him. 'If it is my lord Aimery's wish,' she said in a low voice, 'then of course I will obey.'

Isobel smiled, satisfied. So, this was the way to subjugate the girl! My lord Aimery's wish. What an innocent little fool she was! Lord Aimery, in fact, knew nothing at all about all this, as he had ridden out on the dawn patrol with his men and would not be back till this evening. But how was the Saxon slut to know?

In fact, Isobel had felt a desperately fierce pang of jealousy as she'd entered the room and seen the unclothed girl standing there as if she was in a dream. The sunlight had played magically on her high, perfect breasts, on her slender hips and long legs; on that soft golden fleece at the top of her thighs and the clouds of glorious silken hair cascading round her shoulders.

Isobel vowed anew in that moment that she would subjugate this girl herself, if Aimery would not.

Elena was slowly lifting the rough woollen tunic over her head when Isobel reached out languidly to stroke the exposed, taut skin of her abdomen. Elena gasped and froze; Isobel, with a smile, trailed her fingers towards the juncture of the girl's thighs, where the soft gold hair curled so delicately.

'My dear,' she murmered, 'just like gold silk! So

delicate. Quite, quite charming. But you really do need educating, don't you? So sadly lacking in any refinement. And Aimery really does not care, you know, for unsophisticated women.' Isobel's thumb brushed tantalisingly at the top of Elena's secret place, stroking the pleasure bud, pinching the outer lips swiftly, then withdrawing her hand. Elena gasped and flushed at the sudden burst of pleasure that assailed her, and Isobel laughed at the girl's consternation.

'So,' she went on, 'the lord Aimery has given me something for you. A little gift, if you like. He made it quite clear that he wished you to wear this special garment.'

Elena, her spine tingling with unease, said suddenly, 'Where is lord Aimery?'

'Gone out with his men. He then has to escort a convoy from Lincoln through his territory, so he will not be back for some time. But he left this for you, my dear. Here – let me show you.' And, reaching into the recessed folds of her skirt, she drew out what looked to Elena like a small leather belt.

Elena, still naked, clutched the serf's tunic to her defenceless body, and shivered with apprehension. There was something sinister about the belt that Isobel dangled teasingly before her, with its buckles and straps. 'I would rather not wear it,' she whispered.

Isobel, watching her, felt a renewed surge of hatred. This girl was fresh, young, innocent. *And Aimery had gone to her room last night . . .*

'Oh, dear,' chided Isobel in her sweetest tones.

'Disobedience already! I shall have to tell Aimery – he will be most disappointed in you – '

She saw how the girl's face became drained of blood. She was obviously terrified of Aimery's disapproval. Poor girl, she was besotted, like all the others before her. And therefore well on the way to her downfall . . .

'So, of course,' Isobel went on brightly, 'you will wear the belt, won't you, my dear? Here, let me help you.'

'It is the lord Aimery's wish?' said the girl quietly.

'Of course.'

The girl bit her lip and nodded mutely. With a secret smile of satisfaction, Isobel helped her into the little belt that was one of her own favourite devices. Elena had to step into it because, although the main strap was buckled round her waist, there was a further piece of leather that pulled up tightly between her legs, cradling the soft mound of her femininity, narrowing at the back to slip between the rounded cheeks of her bottom. Elena gasped at the unfamiliar feel of the cold leather against her outer flesh lips. 'It is too tight!'

'Nonsense!' retorted Isobel briskly as she nimbly tightened the big buckle at Elena's small waist, thus drawing up the strap between her legs even further. 'This is how it is meant to be worn. You will soon be perfectly used to it. It is quite customary for favoured female slaves, I assure you!'

She let her fingers trail along the firm leather that pressed against the girl's delicious femininity, secretly revelling in the exquisite combination of soft, tempting flesh and dark, thick leather. The girl, with her stupid, innate modesty, recoiled with a shudder from her touch; but Isobel knew that already the cunningly-made love belt would be doing its work. Because where it pressed against Elena's pink folds it was slightly ridged, so that it would exert gentle yet persistent pleasure on her tender flesh lips. It would eventually part them, chafing against her sweet pleasure zones with every step she took, preparing her for the entertainment that Isobel had in mind for the afternoon.

Already, Isobel could see that the girl was breathing raggedly with the secret combination of shame and promised pleasure. Isobel smiled. 'The lord Aimery will be most pleased to know that you are obeying him,' she lied softly. 'Now I will send my maid Alys, to take you down to the kitchens.'

And with that, the lady Isobel left the room.

Elena stood very still after she had gone, trying desperately to order her reeling thoughts. She would run away from Thoresfield! She would not suffer this humiliation!

Pulling on her coarse woollen gown, she moved purposefully towards the door. The castle gates were open. No-one would notice yet another serf heading off towards the fields.

Suddenly, as she moved, the ridged leather slipped up between her flesh lips and rubbed with heart-stopping sweetness at her secret parts. The delicious warmth, the novel feeling of constriction, flooded her belly, and she felt her nipples tingle suddenly where the woollen gown chafed them.

She remembered Aimery's dark embrace; her body's awakening in his arms. Already, the leather belt was moist between her legs. She moved again, tentatively, towards the door; the leather rubbed softly against that very heart of her pleasure, nudging at the little bud that the Breton had caressed so sweetly last night. Maybe tonight he would come to her again.

Elena knew then that she would not, could not run away. She knew that a day of exquisite torment lay ahead, like a challenge – a challenge issued by the lady Isobel. She drew a deep breath and turned back into her room, to await her next orders.

She would rise to that challenge, and win.

The Gift of Shame

Sarah Hope-Walker

Sarah Hope-Walker has written two Black Lace novels: *The Gift of Shame* and *Unfinished Business*. I have chosen an extract from *The Gift of Shame*, her first book, which tells the story of Helen who not only rediscovers her sexuality after a period of mourning, but meets someone who allows her to explore the darker side of her imagination. The book relishes in the forbidden fun that can be experienced by mutually consenting adults.

The Gift of Shame

She had woken early and stood at the foot of the bed looking down on his sleeping face filled with a sense of wonder.

He looked so vulnerable in repose. No sign of that energy that could prompt searing orgasm in her. She had never imagined such intensity of feeling existed. With Kenneth their love-making had been tender, only pretend daring and adventurous but always neatly compartmentalised, tagged as something the mind turned to at bedtime. Never had she imagined that there could be a passion so all consuming that she wouldn't be able to rid herself of it even when asleep.

Acknowledging that her abstinence since Kenneth's traumatic death had created an almost unbearable pressure, she knew that this was more than the sudden, and finite, release of a bursting dam. Jeffrey had, she suspected, tapped a deep resource and opened her to a continuing, renewable flow.

As she watched him sleep she was afraid that he might wake and find her wanting. What he had to give was so precious it should be given as a tribute to perfection and that, she knew, she was not. What she needed was artifice and the good luck not be found out too soon.

It was as if all that had gone before had been simple preparation. In his presence she had found a fierce pride in her body. Until now it had been appreciated, tenderly kissed and caressed, but never before had she felt it so openly worshipped. With this man she could go confidently naked. With this man she could be openly wanton.

Then, aware that his eyes were open and watching her, she straightened her back, put back her shoulders, and made the best of her pose.

'Come,' he said throwing back the covers to show his risen flesh.

Like a supplicant approaching a holy relic she crawled onto the bed and gratefully did as he wanted.

First she licked, nuzzled and kissed him, and then, carefully, alert to any contrary instruction he might give her, raised her loins to straddle him, and reaching down, guided him into herself.

His intake of breath was all the goad she needed. Now he must be ridden like the thoroughbred he was. First, the trot, then the canter and finally the gallop.

It wasn't until he cried out and grasped her that she realised the flame that had been heating her had come as much from his hands, rhythmically slapping her buttocks, as from the reliquary buried deep between her thighs.

Feeling him gone from the field she lay beside him and wished away the time that would pass before his next arousal.

'What am I to do with you?'

'Anything you want,' she told him.

'You know that I can't let you go?'

'I've nowhere I want to go.'

They lay silently exchanging caresses for a moment before she found the agony of him not being inside her more than she could bear. 'Shall I make some coffee?' she asked.

'I insist,' he said softly, and added a kiss to the breast closest to his mouth.

She reached for his head as tiny darts of flame came from his lips through her nipples to the pleasure places in her brain.

'Coffee,' he said bringing her from her tantalising fantasies.

Reluctantly, she rose from the bed and, in a reflex born of custom, reached for her robe.

'No,' he told her. 'I want you naked.'

She felt inclined to tease him. 'I was always told a woman's body looked better if she was wearing a little something.'

'A man would have to be mad to acquire a perfect Ming vase and then want to cover it with a cloth wouldn't he?'

'Am I your "Ming"?'

'You are exquisite and very precious and beside you a Ming is commonplace.'

She felt liquid with the release from months of remorse and self denial. She wanted to rush at him and re-pledge herself but instead, feeling that she was exercising super-human control, she turned away from the extravagance of his compliment and went into the kitchen.

As she went through the mindless ritual of coffee-making she wished she had something more exotic, something undreamt of, to offer him. But, she wistfully understood, there was only herself – and that, too, was soon to be found out. She had an uneasy feeling that they had started too quickly and, too soon, gone too far. She feared that anything travelling at this velocity must surely come off the rails at the first curve.

Towards noon he was to surprise her yet again.

Ordering her to stay as she was, he produced a pencil and a pad of notepaper and started sketching her. At first she was happy enough to have a reason to stay still for a moment and expected his sketches to be no more than amateur crudities. So she was pleasantly surprised, when he handed them to her, to see a vibrant, naked young woman – one who just happened to have her face – drawn with great economy and directness.

'You're an artist?'

'An early ambition, quickly squashed.'

'What happened?'

'My father. I wanted to go to art school but he insisted that I should study something more voca-tional. The closest to art he would allow was architecture.'

He placed her in another pose and as he worked she thought she had found the first weak spot in his, until now, apparently impregnable armour.

'Isn't it a little unusual to give up art to become a property tycoon?'

'In the first place I haven't given up art. Secondly

I became – what you are pleased to call – a
"property tycoon" by accident. The same father that
denied me my earlier ambitions left me a seedy,
run down, rambling apartment block whose only
asset was a good address. I used my newly acquired
architectural skills to refurbish it. Everyone told me
I was crazy and that it didn't make economic sense,
but I couldn't stand owning anything that was that
shabby and that ugly. Then the controlled rent laws
were changed. I had moved it up market and it
became the collateral asset from which I spread
upward and outward.'

'And what happened to the art?'

He shrugged off the question and only the sound
of his pencil spoilt the absolute silence until he
heaved a huge sigh.

'It's time you knew about me,' he said.

Allowing her only a raincoat and a pair of shoes,
she found herself being hustled out of her apartment to feel the chilly December wind invading
parts she would never have normally exposed to
the winter chill.

'Where are we going?'

'To my place.'

They got to a street corner and he hesitated. She
didn't notice his concern at first. She was too busy
eagerly scanning the faces of passers-by trying to
judge whether or not they could sense she was
naked under the coat. She found it particularly
thrilling when she understood that no one was
noticing. Either that or they just didn't give a damn!

His cursing brought her back to the present
reality.

'The bloody car's gone!' he exploded. 'I wasn't

sure at first but now I distinctly remember parking
it there outside that shop.'

'Stolen?' she asked.

'Or towed away. Come on, we'll have to get a cab.'

He was one of those people for whom taxis
miraculously appeared on cue. It was in the cab
that she was reminded that he loved to play erotic
games.

He urged her to move from the rear seat to the
jump seat directly in front of him. Aware of the taxi
driver just a foot away from her back, she understood the point of the game and moved her thighs
apart allowing the coat to fall away from her legs,
fully exposing herself to him.

He mouthed to her that she should play with
herself and for the first time in his presence she
hesitated. The cab driver couldn't see but she feared
other passing drivers – especially those sitting high
in trucks or buses – might.

'Do it!' he said in a loud authoritative voice that
made the cab driver think his words had been
intended for him.

'Not you, driver!' he yelled back. 'I was talking
to my whore!'

The cab driver chuckled but she was mortally
offended. Snapping her legs together she carefully
drew the coat back over her thighs to cover herself.
She found she couldn't look at him.

'That . . .' he said in a soft even voice, '. . . was
very naughty of you.'

Still refusing to look at him, she stared instead
out of the side window.

Minutes later the cab drew up in front of the
prestigious address that was his flagship property

and she sat tight, undecided whether by going home directly she would be punishing herself more than him. It was then she realised her predicament. If she took the cab home she would have nothing to pay the man with and, then again, wouldn't it be silly to take the one cab driver in London who might guess at her condition and lead him to her home so he would know where she lived?

When Jeffrey offered a hand out of the cab, she took it, telling herself she had no choice.

She still didn't feel like talking to him but was, despite herself, impressed as they crossed the refurbished, somewhat kitsch, lobby towards the elevators.

The receptionist called out a greeting, as did the man in a porter's uniform who hurried from some back room as if anxious to look alert in his employer's eyes.

Once inside the elevator she couldn't help noticing the Yale key he used to unlock the mechanism before it would respond to the PENTHOUSE button. She noted she was with a man who valued his security.

The elevator moved swiftly up but she kept a hurt distance. She felt pained that he made no attempt to break the silence and ask her what was wrong. She knew he didn't have to – that he already knew precisely at which moment the deep freeze had set in and why.

The doors opened into a small lobby and he had to use a magnetic key on a second set of heavy double doors before they would open.

When they did she was treated to an apartment of, literally, breath-taking proportions. It had the dimensions of a hotel lobby but there was little evidence of the over-zealous symmetry which some interior designers imposed. Instead, the main living room was split into groupings of furniture with a profusion of potted, semi-tropical plants that reduced the vast expanse to human proportions.

There were several messages on his answerphone so, in response to his invitation to have a look round, she started on a self-conducted tour.

Everywhere she looked was evidence of abundant affluence. Its corollary – bad taste – was totally absent. Jeffrey had managed to make a display that avoided vulgarity and ostentation. Although it was demonstrably impossible she got the feeling that this apartment had been here for some long time. There was no questioning its modernity but he had gifted it permanence.

She remembered being told how an aristocrat had made a 'put down' remark about someone he considered a parvenu. 'He's the sort of chap that buys his own furniture.'

Jeffrey had done that but avoided being too precise, too matching. She couldn't help noticing that the bed would accommodate four people with comfort. She wondered how many times it had.

When she returned to the living area she heard him telling a girl, his secretary, surely, about the missing car and asking her to take the necessary steps, including informing the police. Did this man do nothing for himself?

When he laid the phone down he turned to her.

'It's a beautiful apartment,' she said.

'So! You've found your voice again!'

'You shouldn't have called me a whore!'

50

'I didn't,' he said, 'call you "a" whore. I called you "my" whore. There's a difference.'

'Well I'm not.'

He shrugged. 'You're free to leave,' he said.

She was standing in front of him, separated from the desk by two metres of velvety carpet. His words had stunned her. She even felt tears beginning to threaten her composure.

'Are you tired of me, then?' she said.

'No, but if you want to play then you play my rules.'

'Don't I get any choice?'

'Only when to stay and when to go. Do you want to go?'

'You know I don't.'

He nodded, stood up and closed the space between them to stand directly in front of her.

'Get rid of that coat and bend over the desk.'

Angry at him and herself for knowing that she would accept this humiliation, she tried to protest, but he cut her short by grabbing her, turning her and almost ripping the coat from her body. As she yelled desperately at him he propelled her forward to the desk and forced her face down to crush her nose into the smell of polished leather.

She opened her mouth to protest again at this treatment, but the word became a cry; then she felt him firmly entering her. Suddenly all protest seemed superfluous. Anger turned to joy as his words battered her ears.

'You disobeyed me in the cab, didn't you?'

'Yes!' she yelled.

'Are you sorry?'

'Yes!'

'Are you going to be my whore?'
'Yes!'
'What happens to disobedient whores?'
'They get fucked over desks!'
'Wrong!' his words seething into her ears like liquid lava. 'They get punished!'
'Yes! Punish me, screw me! Do anything you like to me!'
And then, in unison, they came.

Later that evening she stood tied loosely between two posts. Her feet firmly on the ground and though not strained she was, nevertheless, tethered, as immobile and fearful as any creature awaiting an unknown fate.

He had come to her and, without explanation, tied her wrists together with a silken cord. Then leading her to stand between the posts, had first tied her and then gently fed a knotted bandana into her mouth to silence her.

Without a word of explanation, not a look, nor a backward glance, he had left her among the ornamental plants that crowded for space in his heated solarium as if she was just another passive ornament among the many. The worst moment came when he turned off the lights in the solarium leaving her with only the incidental light escaping from the living area.

She had been there for what seemed to her an eternity. Her thoughts were confused by the dull ache that had started in her raised arms but one message repeated and repeated until she was sure it would become engraved on her throat. She hated him. Hated this. The moment she was released, it was over. How dare he do this to her? How dare he assume that there could possibly be any pleasure for her in such humiliation?

If he had stayed, if he had watched her, it might have become marginally supportable, interesting even, but she could hear him somewhere in the apartment making phone calls – arranging to go to a New Year's Eve party – and then, worst of all she could hear the drone of the TV.

Deep in her discomfort she tortured herself with the thought that she knew very little of this man . . . that wealth did not prevent someone being mad – only from being locked up. Suppose he was a maniac and intended to kill her? There was nothing she could do about it!

Hate him! Hate this! It's over between us!

She saw him coming and watched, her face muscles tensing, her vocal cords rehearsing the invective she intended showering on him. Punishment? He didn't know the meaning of the word.

'So, are you suitably chastened?'

His finger tips reached out and gently touched her nipples. It was as if he had touched her with heated needles.

The hands moved outward and encircled her breasts. His lips nestled to her throat, from which she couldn't escape. His hands circled her belly and then gently, with the subtlety of a soldering iron, touched her most vulnerable bud of flesh.

Then a switch was thrown and a gear moved in her body. She found herself moaning, pressing herself against his caresses, and desperately wanting him. But please God, she thought, first, please, set me free!

'I love you like this.'

God. No. Not like this! Please don't let me come!

His fingers returned to her nipples, now extended and sensitive. Gently at first he tweaked them then, increasing the pressure, he bit his nails into her tender flesh.

Using one hand he reached up and loosened the silk gag, and threw it from them.

'I want to see you smile,' he said, increasing the nail-given pain.

She was breathing too hard, her throat too dry to say anything.

'If you smile for me and tell me you love me then I'll set you free.'

Her uncertain eyes managed to still his swimming image and she saw his eyes – those eyes! Then, straining every muscle in her face, she managed to smile. 'I love you,' she said.

It was late evening before they spoke of anything other than their pleasure.

'Why did you do that to me?'

'You deserved it.'

'Why did you just leave me there and walk away?'

'I had things to do.'

'I hated you. You know that, don't you?'

He smiled to himself and by doing so rekindled the anger he had washed away with a gesture.

'I think I still hate you.'

'That's healthy. Hate is closer to love than any other emotion.'

Earlier he had shown her the tanning lamps built into the solarium to bring a touch of summer to even the dreariest winter's day.

They now lay side by side enjoying the counter-feit sun.

'Are you frightened?' he asked her.

'I'm not sure. I think I am but it's like a recurring nightmare. You know it will come at you in the night but it doesn't stop you wanting to go to sleep.'

'I have a technique for destroying nightmares. What you do is turn and face them. Stops the pursuing horror dead in its tracks. When you know your fear you can face it.'

'That's how I feel about you. Unknown. And yes, that frightens me.'

'Sure it isn't yourself that frightens you? Haven't you found out things about yourself you never knew?'

'Also.'

Even as she spoke she discovered something new about herself. She could lie here next to him and calmly, objectively, discuss things which would have, previously, shamed her in any context other than the throes of passion. Of course the protective eye shields they were wearing helped. The past few days had taught her that direct eye contact can be the most excoriating experience between two people.

Warmed by the lamps, confident to be naked yet masked from the world, she felt totally relaxed.

'What do you want of me?' she asked him out of a lengthening silence.

'To be allowed to worship.'

'Worship what?'

'You.'

'Is that what you think you were doing when you tied me up in the solarium?'

In truth she still harboured a hate of what he had done to her but also recognised that there was emerging a perverse recognition that the price was worth it for the joyous aftermath. When he had finally released her, the pain, if anything, had increased. The blood rushing back into her veins had seemed loaded with liquid fire rendering her totally helpless – and therefore without responsibility – for what had followed – an unfathomable depth of pleasure.

He had stayed silent for a long moment. 'Do you know how incredibly beautiful you looked?'

'How could I?' she asked with a degree of asperity.

'You're right,' he said. 'There should have been a mirror. Selfish of me. Next time. Promise.'

'What makes you think there'll be a next time?'

'There won't,' he said. 'Unless you want it.'

This struck her as a bizarre remark and left her feeling curiously bereft. Must she be forced to ask him to torture her? Did he imagine she ever would?

At that moment the timer that controlled the ultraviolet dosage clicked off and broke the mood.

Lifting the shields from their eyes they looked at each other as if for the very first time. Curiously, she even felt a little shy.

'Say it,' he said. 'Say the words you have often thought but have never dared say to a lover.'

The challenge struck her to the core. The words were there instantly, known to her since puberty and although never spoken they were now brazenly echoing in her mind and insisting she give them life. Words that, if she spoke them, would be the most terrible of all her betrayals of Kenneth. Fight as she might she couldn't stop them as they leapt into life from her lips.

'Fuck me in the arse,' she said and, unable to take breath until he answered, she listened, horrified, to the dying echo of the words.

Had he laughed. Had he leapt on her and taken her cruelly in that place where she knew she would suffer, she might have been able to plead a moment of madness, but he didn't. Instead he held her eyes for a whole heart-stopping minute then, standing, he reached down a hand to help her to her feet. 'Come with me,' he said softly.

Now quite frightened by what she might have started she padded beside him across the wide carpet and into his bedroom.

Throwing open his closets he indicated the rank upon rank of suits, shirts, ties and underwear.

'If you are to be taken like a man you will dress like one. You have one hour before I greet your identical twin brother.'

Turning, he left her alone with a heart-pounding dread at what she had done. Damn him, she thought. Why couldn't he have just taken her? Why force her into this humiliating ritual and make her responsible for her own madness?

If she did as he asked there was no escape, no turning back, no excuses she could make to herself in some future sleepless night. She was alone with her own wantonness.

Finding a full-length mirror she questioned her reflection. 'Shall you be his whore?'

After a moment's pause the image in the mirror, eyes wild with light, smiled and nodded.

The Artist-In-Residence

Sophia Mortensen

Sophia Mortensen is a new writer whose work immediately made itself apparent as being suitable for the series. Her short story, *The Artist-in-Residence* is a delightful and very rude account of what happens when a young woman with fetishistic tendencies gets a placement in the educational wing of a religious establishment. The potential for leading lots of young men astray is enormous!

The Artist-In-Residence

Caroline had been artist-in-residence at St Joseph's college scarcely six weeks before the trouble started. It all began, as so many misdemeanours do, in the library. It was Friday afternoon and the pale November sun cast a watery light over the desks as assorted members of the clergy went about their business with silent efficiency. Caroline was sitting at a desk facing the entrance to the library and was busy scribbling notes for her forthcoming paper on the role of women in religious painting.

A weighty, leather-bound encyclopaedia of art history lay in front of her, open at a section on Gustave Moreau. His work had captured her attention earlier that year, in the closing weeks of her time at art school. The sinister beauty of his Salome in *The Apparition* and the tortured, androgynous figures in his painting *The Suitors* excited in her a feeling that was positively voluptuous. The complexity of the work was mesmeric, the painterly

61

skill impressive, but it was the women in his pictures which impressed her the most.

Not for Moreau the fluttering fairy creatures of Romanticism; Moreau's women were deadly beings whom it would be unwise to upset. They exuded a cruel majesty which Caroline aspired to. She sat admiring the colour plates, imagining herself in the role of Jupiter, dressed for nothing other than pleasure – but pleasure not given lightly.

How Caroline loathed having to wear respectable day clothes. Her postgraduate study here at St Joseph's required conservative dress as this small, educational place of worship offered places only to those who chose to pursue a theological career. Caroline had worked hard for a placement in a religious establishment and wasn't about to put her aspirations in jeopardy by flouting their old-fashioned codes of conduct. To compensate, however, she had taken to wearing undergarments of unusual design. After having tried on a corset in a theatrical costumiers in London for her fancy dress graduation party earlier that year, Caroline had realised that her taste for garments of constriction was somewhat more enthusiastic than that of other girls her age. At twenty five, she was pretty and not afflicted by false modesty. Her waist-length chestnut hair, naturally shiny, hung like a glossy curtain down her back and when curled and pinned up to stunning effect looked beautifully sculptured. Her nicely-rounded form invited contemplation; while in no way skinny, her limbs were graceful and well proportioned and her breasts – although small – were immediately noticeable as pert mounds underneath her jumper. Most striking, however, was her face. Her dark eyebrows arched quizzically over deep-brown, heavily-lashed eyes and her lips were full and rose-coloured, looking for all the world as if they had been anointed with berry juice. Not for Caroline the countenance of the cynical art student, nor the insiped pallor of one who has spent too long in a darkroom. Her face exuded a healthy glow, and brightness shone from within her.

Her secret wardrobe was coming together quite nicely. With little to do at nights save more studying or venturing into town with students of a devout religious persuasion – who were, she thought, all unattractive – she would find sanctuary in her room by transforming herself from smartly-dressed academic to tightly-corseted mistress, experimenting with her hair and make-up and preparing for the inevitable day when –

Her reverie was interrupted as the arrival of a visiting party punctured the library's respectful silence.

'If you care to look, gentlemen, the library at St Joseph's boasts a collection of religious art books unparalleled in other colleges,' announced the elderly rector, his voice becoming louder as they approached the entrance. 'Feel free to browse, should any of you have an interest in religious art, otherwise we shall continue our tour along the main vestibule of the annexe.'

Several pairs of polished shoes creaked on the heavily varnished wooden floor and Caroline was forced to look up from her book. From where she was seated, she could spot Father Benedict addressing his troop, who were obscured from her vision by a ceiling-high bank of library shelves. He was an enthusiastic host and always showing parties of old clergymen around St Joseph's. She would probably be asked to give another lecture; to engage once more in gentle hyperbole with octogenarians. She sighed. To be surrounded each day by elderly and celibate men was nothing short of cruel. It seemed a shame that her postgraduate placement had to mean abstention from the pleasures of flirtation. During her undergraduate years, Caroline had indulged in games of lascivious courtship with enthusiasm.

She heard a voice; the first to engage in conversation with their host. 'And does the college have any paintings in its collection? Say, those of Burne-Jones or Holman-Hunt, perhaps? I've heard that some of the Pre-Raphaelite works are in private collections.'

It was then, with great pleasure, that Caroline realised her first impression had been very wrong. For the average age of the rector's visiting party was at least 55 years younger than she had predicted. She caught a glimpse of them through gaps in the shelves as they continued their stroll to the opposite end of the room. Who were they, this group of young men? Maybe they were other art students visiting St Joseph's for research purposes for their dissertations. But no. She'd already heard the rector ask them if they were interested in art. If they were from a visiting art school – as she had been, this time last year – that question would be redundant. She assumed they were all male, so it was unlikely they were students. Female art students outnumbered males by four to one.

She had to find out who they were. She swivelled around in her chair and waited as the party emerged at the other end of the room. They continued their walk towards her. As they approached, she noticed their clothes looked somewhat irregular for students unless – of course! Realisation dawned on her with great disappointment. They were trainee priests; young men sworn to the cloth.

The visiting party continued their tour of the library, crossing the room to look at some of the exhibits on view in glass cases, illuminated manuscripts and the like, all the while getting a running commentary from Father Benedict. Caroline carefully observed them from a distance. Ever aware of aesthetics, she noted with immediate approval, the appearance of one of them. At an age when young men are meant to be in their sexual prime, this poor chap was practising vows of celibacy. The sight of this beautiful young creature, clad in the sombre garments of his chosen calling stirred feelings in Caroline which provoked an immediate response. She felt herself begin to moisten as impure thoughts flashed into her mind. The dew which soaked into her oyster-coloured silk knickers felt warm and viscous. If there was such a thing as a lust gland, Caroline's was working overtime. As her beauty lips engorged with desire, her gold labial piercing twisted itself around to gently graze her clitoris. She softly squeezed her legs together and wriggled on the seat. It would be enough to bring her off right there in the library, should she continue her hidden writhings while observing this delightful creature from a concealed distance – like some kind of academic voyeur. How old was he? she thought.

No older than twenty-three, surely. His countenance resembled that of a petulant child. His expression would have looked more at home on a reform-school boy than an aspiring man of the cloth. His pale hair flopped forward over his forehead, his complexion looked baby-soft and on the end of his nose there rested a pair of round gold-rimmed glasses which added a curious intelligence to the petulance. The long black gown which covered his body from neck to feet concealed, she surmised, an athletic structure: a body which would never know the delights of a woman's ministrations, she pondered with regret.

They had finished looking at whatever it was Father Benedict was showing them and started to walk towards where Caroline was seated. She fidgeted, trying to remain impervious to the presence of the beautiful one.

'This is Miss Caroline Wardell,' informed Father Benedict, 'whose outstanding academic achievement in the subject of religious art has earned her a year's placement in our educational department. During your stay here, you may bump into Caroline in the course of your studies in the library, or in the chapel where she sketches the statues occasionally. Isn't that right, my dear?' he asked.

'Oh, absolutely. I'm already finding my time here most rewarding, Father,' she replied, squirming in her chair, fixing her gaze on the young blond man. She was scared to move from her chair. She felt so wet inside her panties, she was worried that her skirt may have darkened and if she stood up, this group of holy men would know her terrible secret.

Every pair of eyes was on her and all of them

were male. Despite her concern about her over-active juices, she felt a curious sense of triumph. There is nothing like dominion to give one a sense of power, thought Caroline. Being the only young female in the building, she was unhindered by all-too-knowing creatures of the same sex. For men, Caroline had long been aware, were remarkably easy to affect and manipulate.

She found herself looking straight into the eyes of the object of her increasing desire. She had singled out the gorgeous one and had only a couple of moments by which to impress herself upon his consciousness. He certainly looked the most artistic of the group; the others looked somewhat gauche, ungainly and not at ease with themselves in the same way as he was. Her agile mind decided to take a chance and in the second before Father Benedict was about to announce their departure, she blurted out, 'Did I hear one of you ask some-thing about Burne-Jones?' Without waiting for a reply she continued, 'My dissertation last year was on the subject of Pre-Raphaelite women.' She looked around at the whole group, so as not to be quite so obvious in her attentions. Luck appeared to be on her side. Her intuition rarely let her down.

'Yes,' came a quiet but assured reply from the young man. 'I find an exquisite sense of peace from contemplating the masterly skill of Pre-Raphaelite work and, well, they're something of an obsession of mine,' he continued, smiling shyly.

An obsession! Priests weren't meant to have obsessions, thought Caroline. The rest of the group seemed restless. They had obviously heard it all before.

'I see young Gregory has found something of an ally,' said Father Benedict, cheerfully. 'Come, let us continue our tour. Gregory, we'll be heading towards the annexe for refreshments. Join us at your leisure.' And with that, the rest of the group dispersed.

Caroline was thinking fast. Her agile mind had not known such a challenge since attending her placement interview. With his colleagues out of the way, they were practically alone together. He was obviously a little nervous about this. Caroline realised it was time to take control; to work her charm with skill. 'I would very much like to show you what I've written on the subject,' she announced, 'if you were interested.' She took care to maintain a regal air. If it sounded like she was showing off, she didn't care. 'This term, I'm studying Symbolist allegory within religious painting,' she said.

She paused, placing her pen on her lower lip, making minute movements around its tip with her tongue. She was aware of how her every action was under scrutiny from her sex-starved audience of one. 'St Joseph's is wonderfully ... equipped,' she added.

Caroline let her gaze wander from his eyes, and down the length of his body. She knew that under his priestly robes there was a pounding and delightful gift, waiting and wanting her to release it from its capacious covering. If only you knew what was happening between my legs, you wouldn't feel so alone, she thought. She cursed Catholicism and the guilty baggage which accompanied it. She wanted to introduce young Gregory to sinful pleasure. But she had to hurry. 'I would be delighted to tell you all about my studies for the particular paper I'm preparing. But do let me know if I'm boring you. I do go on sometimes.' She could tell from the young man's shaky hands and dry lips the effect she was having. She was so quietly yet so powerfully sexual when she wanted to be: when she needed to be.

'No. No, not at all,' said Gregory. 'I would be delighted to see your writing, especially your dissertation. I am always keen to learn new things about my chosen areas of interest.'

'Oh, me too,' replied Caroline. She arranged to meet him later, in the small church, where a practice communion was being conducted at seven o'clock.

Caroline couldn't face the boredom of another service and besides, she wanted time to prepare for her rendezvous. Once satisfied with her ensemble, she slipped her coat on and made her way to the chapel just before eight. She was slightly early. Trainee conmmunion had finished and Gregory was folding the altar cloth with reverence. The others had left to prepare for supper and the chapel was silent. Caroline's entrance startled the young man. He whirled round, and stood aghast as a female image of the kind he had only dared dream of walked towards him.

Caroline was dressed very differently from how she had been earlier, in the library. Over a thin, cream silk blouse she wore a severe-looking and waist-clinching leather corset which pushed her firm breasts upwards and made them even more noticeable. Her skirt was long and dark and would have looked conservative if not for the fact that the buttons on the front of the garment, from her hem to halfway up her thighs, were undone and exposing a lot of leg. Gregory's eyes darted from her breasts to the uppermost area of her thighs. He could just see the lacy tops of her stockings and a tiny amount of flesh. Soft, warm, womanly flesh. He was so startled that his calculated, ritualistic tidying of the altar changed immediately to fumbling clumsiness. His pale hair flopped in front of his eyes and he could barely get up the courage to address her. After several drawn-out seconds of agonised silence, he managed to stammer a hello.

'You look nice,' he said, almost inaudibly, his nerves making him feel thirsty and weak.

'I feel nice, Gregory,' she replied, looking him straight in the eyes. She took the communion goblet from him and placed it back on the altar. She took one of his hands to her lips and gently kissed it, then allowed it to follow its natural course – towards her silk-covered bosom. His face reddened, his eyes were downcast and he was trembling.

'I have to wait for Father Richard,' he said. 'It's my turn to be in charge of the altar today and my punctuality and adherence to discipline is being monitored. Regretfully, I think I'll have to decline your earlier invitation,' he stuttered.

Caroline could see he was worried but it didn't stop her from getting slightly annoyed at him for being so subservient to the priesthood; so in awe of religious doctrine. She was going to have to be firm if she was to get her way with this young man. 'It's not an invitation, Gregory,' Caroline said firmly. 'It's an order. I noticed the way you were looking at me earlier in the library.' She leaned closer and grabbed him by the arm, pressing him firmly against the altar. She slipped her right leg between his legs, trapping him with her thighs. With her right hand she lightly traced a path towards the centre of his body; an area as yet untouched by woman. She smiled as she felt his hardness and she moistened. 'You're supposed to be sworn to celibacy very soon, my dear. This could be your last and only chance to spend an evening in the company of a normal woman. Think about it,' she added, coquettishly. 'I won't tell a soul.'

'I'm not experienced. I . . . I don't know much, well, anything really.'

'Don't worry. *I* do,' whispered Caroline into his ear. She continued to rub her hand along the dark cloth of his priestly robes. His penis felt huge and hot inside its confines.

In a moment of temptation too strong to resist, Gregory consented and allowed her to lead him from the chapel, around the back of the building, and up to the residents' rooms. The halls of residence were deserted, as was his place at the supper table. Caroline wasted no time. She marched him along the corridor and unlocked the door to her room. Although modestly furnished, it was lavishly adorned and reproductions of Symbolist and religious paintings hung on the walls. A large pencil drawing of Salome holding the head of John the Baptist featured over her bed and reproductions of Moreau's decadent couplings lit up the walls. A look of apprehension crossed young Gregory's face as he swiftly realised he had entered the chamber of some kind of Jezebel. But the pent-up desire of a catalogue of unreleased fantasies swirled around his head and in the presence of such masterful command, he was powerless to resist.

'Take that ridiculous cape off,' she commanded. 'What's the point of dressing up if you're not allowed to have fun.'

'I've not met a girl like you before,' said Gregory. 'I think you're very pretty but I'm not sure I want to go through with this. To think that I've sinned in the house of God.'

'Oh shut up, and stop being pathetic,' said Caroline. She pulled him over to her dressing table and forced him to look in the mirror. 'Look at yourself. Look how attractive you are.' She took off his glasses and ruffled his hair. 'You'll not regret coming here, I assure you,' she said and eased him down on to the bed. She took her coat off and paraded in front of him. Then, slowly, she eased her skirt down over her hips and let it fall to the floor. She stood beside the bed and slipped her hand into her black, lacy knickers and began to touch herself. She was wet and excited although she maintained a calm exterior. She knew that her behaviour would have an immediate effect on the young priest, but if he were to leave now she couldn't bear it. She was too far gone in her arousal. She was going to have to play this very carefully. He lay on her bed, continuing to look nervous but unable to take his eyes off her.

'What do you want me to do?' he asked.

'Turn over,' she ordered.

'What? Why?'

'I said turn over,' she repeated, her irritation and desire inflaming her determination. Briefly he ran his hand over her leather corset. She could see he was fascinated by the material but was too shy to ask if he could touch it properly. She smiled and, once more, indicated for him to turn over. He obeyed, rolling over onto his stomach. As a precaution against him escaping, should he suddenly be consumed with guilt, she took a length of sash cord from the box of tricks stored under her bed and began to bind his hands together.

'Why are you doing this to me? I want to explore you fully. There is no need to tie my hands together,' he protested. But Caroline did not want to hear useless protestations and immediately gagged him with one of her scarves.

'Now you're going to be quiet as you have no choice,' she announced triumphantly. She pulled him up off the bed, wrapped her arms around him and pressed her body against him. He groaned softly, from behind his gag.

'I know that you are a filthy-minded young man because I can feel that you are in a state of excitement,' she said with relish, feeling the hot promise of his hardness through the dark cloth of his trousers. 'And I'm sure that Father Richard and Father Benedict would be most disapproving if they knew what you were doing now,' she continued. 'Indeed, you had better come up with a good excuse for your absence at dinner.'

Gregory whimpered a protest, but by now she had released his stiff prick from its confines and was working it with practised skill as she looked him fully in the eyes. It was a beauty indeed.

His gaze was averted; he couldn't bear to see his own arousal witnessed by someone else; a young, attractive woman at that. Oh the shame was too much to bear! His pious pretensions were dispatched to the realms of ridicule as he blushed and moaned and made pathetic attempts to struggle. Caroline snapped him out of his self-pity.

'I'm going to spare you your virginity and not demand that you perform for me,' Caroline said. 'For I have something even more exciting for you which I know you will like and I'll bet we both get lots of pleasure from.'

She eased him back down on to the bed, untied his hands then demanded that he kneel on all fours with his face turned to the wall. She took another scarf from her dressing table and blindfolded her errant charge. After a few seconds she returned and began to remove his trousers, gently easing them over his enormous hard-on. When they were pulled down to his knees it was then that the full horror of this shameful situation made itself apparent to young Gregory. As she applied a liberal amount of lubricant between his buttocks he knew his fate was sealed. He wasn't going to be made to fuck her. He was going to get a buggering!

Caroline was already wearing the strap-on dildo as she took up her position behind him. How wonderfully alive and powerful she felt watching this young supplicant in the throes of his debauching. His blond hair was getting very messed up each time she forced his face down on to the pillow. He still made small protests into his gag but he was as stiff as a pikestaff and not far from his release. With gentle coaxing she eased the solution into him with her finger, a centimetre at a time until he was sufficiently lubricated. Then, after taking aim, her latex appendage pointed at his virgin bottom-hole, she plunged her six inches into the trainee priest. He yelped in surprise and groaned with a mixture of discomfort, protest and shame; an unholy trinity of violation.

'I know you want to come, you little slut,' she teased, 'but not until I've give you a good seeing-to. You must be made to respect the female; to know her presence is divine and that she is beyond reproach. You can worship your Blessed Virgin all you like, but the devil woman is much more fun. And the words of the song are true, you know; she's going to get you from behind.' Caroline laughed and continued her thrusting.

The north wind puffed a cool breeze through the slightly open window and Caroline felt victorious. There was nothing she preferred to this moment. The shame – the dishonour of this obstinate would-be parson fed her with an energy she found revitalising. She was a champion of depravity at last! His young body, never before violated in this way, was hers for the next few moments. She intended to enjoy it.

Being forced to kneel on all fours, he was unable to give himself the release he craved so fiercely. Caroline sensed his urgency and – although a cruel temptress – was not so cruel as to not let him have his own pleasure. But his release would be in the form of his own debasement, she decided. She stopped lunging into him for a moment and whispered in his ear, 'If you promise not to yell, I'll let you have what you want.'

He nodded his head furiously and she knew she had him in her power. She untied the scarves from the back of his head and gently eased out of him.

He turned around to face her; his cheeks crimson with embarrassment, his breathing fast and shallow. He found the courage to quietly ask, 'Please may I make love to you?'

'What?' Caroline exclaimed. 'Your impertinence is astonishing. To think that you have the gall to expect that I would allow you the indulgence of that which is only permitted in the sanctity of marriage! Oh no, my lad. I want to see your virgin sperm leaving your filthy prick.' She unstrapped the dildo and threw it aside then began to rub herself slowly through her knickers. Gregory's prick was straining and purple and she knew there would be little point in allowing him to fuck her. 'Play with yourself like you do when you're alone,' she ordered.

'How do you know I do that?' he asked, kneeling up on the bed.

'Just call it female intuition,' she replied. He clasped his hand around his huge penis and slowly began to work it up and down.

Caroline moistened her lips with her tongue and, as she watched him, felt her own arousal building to a point of no return. She had resisted the temptation to masturbate earlier, as she prepared herself for their liaison – and Gregory's inevitable fate. She often got really turned on when dressing up for sex – when the excitement was just too much. Sometimes, it was such a wonderful bother being a girl! She could feel her orgasm beginning to build in her thighs and spread quickly upwards to the centre of her being. She made Gregory watch her and slowed her movements to an almost unbearably enticing speed.

'Stop,' she commanded, grabbing hold of his hand. 'I want you to watch me come first. It's my privilege as your mistress for the night.'

Just a couple more gentle touches and her sex began its exquisite dance inside her panties. She was coming, although the only obvious sign was the rapturous expression on her face. She threw back her head and gasped with pleasure. Gregory watched in fascinated awe. The pangs of guilt had long since abated and his whole body felt alive with new sensations. There was no going back. He had to experience what Caroline had just experienced.

'Please, please may I c-come now?' he pleaded, although he found it difficult to say the word.

'OK, Gregory,' she replied, gently. 'But keep your eyes closed and do it slowly. I'm going to watch every second of your most intimate moment.' There was one thing left for Caroline to do in order to complete the task she had set herself earlier. Still recovering from her orgasm, she carefully leaned back and took her camera out from underneath the bed. It was all ready, with flashlight in place and shutter speed correctly set. She concealed it behind her, in case the young priest would be tempted to open his eyes. 'Keep your eyes closed, my sweet. You look wonderful,' she said.

'I can't stop it, Caroline. I'm going to do it now. I'm going to come all over you. Oh Blessed saints, forgive me,' he cried as he spurted his virgin tribute over her bed and onto his priestly robes. With all the skill of a wildlife photographer, she captured him at the Zen instant – the moment of his climax.

* * *

Ten minutes later, they lay together on Caroline's bed. She gently stroked his arm and he remained silent but content, his lovely hair tumbling over the pillow. So it was true what was written in those filthy magazines, thought Gregory. It really was as if flashing lights exploded inside your head when it happened. It had never been as powerful before, when he did it by himself. He wanted that feeling again. He turned to Caroline and whispered, 'Can I come to your room again? I'm here for another two weeks and I'd very much like to make love to you properly, if I may. I would also still like to read your dissertation.'

She smiled. Yes. She'd like that very much. Perhaps they would meet in the chapel after dark and slip into the confessional. She was already concocting fiendish plans. 'Oh I'll have to look at my diary, Gregory,' she said, feigning disinterest. 'You had better return to your room now, though. Sharing with the others, I think they'd notice if you didn't return at all.'

He gathered himself together, polishing his glasses and adjusting his trousers. He was already conjuring up untruths as to his absence at the supper table. It was no good. He realised that he was already on the road to unholy behaviour, even if he had retained his virginity. What a dilemma! He slipped out of her room after planting several kisses on Caroline's lips at her insistence. As he tiptoed down the corridor, he couldn't help grinning to himself.

Before retiring to bed that night, Caroline sat up, admiring herself in the mirror. Another one saved from a life of boredom she thought, smugly. And this time she would have something else to show for it. For her photographic evidence would provide the basis for a stunning new work to be unveiled in the church gallery on the presentation of her master's degree. I think I'll call it *Led Into Temptation*, she thought, smiling sweetly, unpinning her hair and allowing it to cascade around her shoulders.

Crash Course

Juliet Hastings

Juliet Hastings has written four books for Black Lace. This extract from her first title in the series, *Crash Course*, tells what happens when Kate, a bright, young management consultant, has to run a training course at short notice. Three of the four participants are attractive, powerful men and Kate takes the opportunity to train them in a most unorthodox way.

She also writes short stories, mainly with a historical flavour. *The Gilded Cage* is a specially commissioned story for *Pandora's Box* and is set against the exciting and unusual backdrop of 11th century Constantinople: a time of handmaidens and Turkish delight!

Juliet's other Black Lace novels are: *Aria Appassionata* (contemporary London), *White Rose Ensnared* (15th century – during the time of the Wars of the Roses) and (to be published in July 1996) *Forbidden Crusade* (set in the Holy land in 1160).

Crash Course

*A*t least the hotel was up to scratch. Kate preferred to run courses at quiet, luxurious venues, where everything was conducive to concentration, and on this occasion the administrators had done well. The hotel was an old house, comfortable and intimate, with training rooms that were almost like the sort of study you would find within a Victorian rectory. Because the rooms were quite small and there were many of them it was also very private, which suited her plans well.

The hotel manager took her finally to the health suite. 'We have spent a lot of money here,' he said. 'A large pool, as you see: jacuzzi, sauna, steam room, a fully equipped gym and aerobic studio. I'm sure there's everything that your delegates will need.'

I can think of a few things that are missing, Kate smiled to herself, but I've brought them with me. She nodded to the manager and said, 'Can you arrange for me to have exclusive use of the suite?'

'I should think so,' he agreed.

'Please book it for Thursday, that's the final day of the course. And private dining facilities throughout, if they're not already arranged.'

She left the manager and went up to her room. The participants had all arrived and Kate had met them in reception and given them their briefing. They were due to meet in the bar at 6 p.m. for informal introductions. There was just time to do a little last minute revision before the course started.

Kate felt nervous, which surprised her. She had everything planned and she was certain, well, fairly certain, that nothing could go wrong. After a moment she realised that the quivering sensation in the pit of her stomach was not just nerves, but also excitement, sexual excitement. She went quickly across to the bed, pulling off her loose sweater and unbuttoning her jeans: time to dress. Jeans looked fine and gave a relaxed, informal feel, but she wanted something that would indicate that she was in authority. She already had the feeling that she would need it.

She chose a linen shirt dress in a neutral shade and sandals with a slight heel. It looked cool, comfortable and controlled. She thought of putting her hair up, tried it, considered the effect and in the end decided that she preferred it swinging loose, just brushing her shoulders. She wanted to look feminine: she wanted the men to find her attractive. After all, she had every intention of having sex with all of them before the end of the course. She looked at herself in the long mirror with approval. The dress skimmed over her breasts, just hinting at their fullness, and was belted at her narrow waist; then the skirt flared out over her ripe plump hips, giving her an hourglass silhouette. She knew that she looked attractive, excited and eager. Her skin was lightly tanned and flushed with pink and her full lips glistened appealingly. She blew herself a kiss in the mirror and whispered, 'Irresistible.'

The thought of the three men waiting for her downstairs, unaware of what she had in mind for them, made her shiver. She went quickly over to the small suitcase by the bed and opened it, looking down at the contents and breathing fast.

Over the weekend she and David had put together a 'library of training materials', things she thought she might find useful. There were clothes made of silk and lace, leather and rubber, for women and men. There was a whip with a thick handle of plaited leather and a long, soft lash, and a paddle covered with velvet. Beneath the clothes lay several pairs of cuffs and lengths of fine chain, some covered in soft fabric, some glittering metal. And at the very bottom lay a selection of books of erotica, a small glass bottle of fine scented oil and a selection of artificial phalluses, several sizes, made of smooth plastic and burnished wood and even carved and polished stone.

Kate hesitated for a moment, then picked up one of the larger phalluses and carried it across to the desk in the corner of her room, where the participants' profiles were spread out. She unbuttoned her dress and slid the smooth, cold head of the wooden phallus beneath the fabric of her panties. As she looked over each page she rubbed the silky wood very gently against her stiffening clitoris, drawing in her breath through her teeth.

The first picture was of the director's protégé, the smart alec MBA. It was the picture she had looked at in David's flat: a sharp-featured, attractive face, high cheekboned and lean, with tanned skin and gleaming blue eyes beneath dark brows. Kate remembered that face well from a brief encounter in the hotel lobby: its owner was quite tall, slender but muscular, quick and energetic in his movements. She looked again at the picture and put the name to it: Nick. He was very attractive, so much so that she felt a warm dampness gathering between her legs. She pulled her panties down to her ankles and nudged the bulging head of the wooden phallus between the moist lips of her sex. It was thick, and she was not quite wet enough for it to enter her easily; she returned to stroking the little stiff bud of her clitoris and turned to the written comments.

'Don't get the hots for him,' she said aloud to herself. 'Look at that profile. Boy, does he need training!' She read the comments and shook her head.

Nick is very goal-orientated and a high achiever. He is intelligent and quite capable of undertaking even the most complex projects. However, he tends to be overly aggressive with both staff and clients. He has poor listening skills and is intolerant of other people's points of view. These traits will prevent him from making further progression. They have been discussed with him but he rejects them. I expect the course to make him aware of the need for improvement.

On a separate page was a note of what the participant hoped to get out of the course. The box was quite large, but it was filled with two words only in a spiky, aggressive hand: *Fuck knows*.

'Oh dear, oh dear,' murmured Kate, pressing the slippery head of the dildo against her aching vulva. Nick would clearly be a challenge to her abilities as a trainer. But he was so attractive, *so* attractive. She wondered what his body would be like: smooth or hairy, muscled or slender? Would he be a good lover? Egotistical, aggressive men were sometimes magnificent performers, always trying to prove something to themselves: but sometimes they were just plain selfish.

She moved on to the next sheet. From the photograph she saw a big man, wide-shouldered and heavily built, with short wiry hair and a subdued, shadowed face that Kate found strangely sensual. Christopher, she thought. She tried to remember him: her mind contained an image of physical size and quiet watchfulness, and a pair of deep-set, smouldering dark eyes. The whole was oddly disturbing. Reading the notes she found that Christopher's boss found him difficult to manage, opaque and unreadable. 'You never know where you are with him,' said the notes. 'A riddle inside a mystery inside an enigma.'

An enigma, Kate thought. Well, she would try to find out what he was like underneath his expensive clothes. Although he was so big he had not seemed actually threatening, but she imagined that anyone with that amount of raw physical power could be frightening on occasion. I will handle you with kid gloves, Christopher, she thought. She imagined that broad-shouldered, heavy body naked, that strange, sensual face looming above her. If a man that big took it into his mind to do something to her, anything, she would not be able to stop him. The thought made her squirm and she tried again to insert the wooden phallus into her aching vagina. She was very wet now and after a little resistance it slipped in easily, filling her deliciously. She squeezed at the slick wood with her inner muscles and leant back a little in the chair, very gently touching her clitoris with her other hand. She was imagining Christopher's big body poised over her as David had sat over Natalie, strong thighs spread on either side of her head, holding one of her wrists in each hand so that she could not struggle. She kicked with her legs and moaned in delirious protest while he thrust deeply into her helpless mouth with his taut, thick penis. The shadowy forms of the other participants loomed in her imagination, two of them stooping to lick her nipples while beautiful dark Nick took hold of her ankles and quelled her struggles and spread her thighs wide, then leant forward and pushed his eager shaft inside her. As the thick wooden phallus slid to and fro, faster and faster, Kate could almost hear Nick gasping as he drove into her and feel the skin of Christopher's abdomen tautening as he approached his climax, his cock thrusting so deep into her mouth that the velvety glans touched the back of her throat. As her orgasm brimmed up and filled her she plunged the wooden phallus deep, deep into her moist love passage, and her fingers worked busily between her legs. At the moment of climax she imagined Nick jerking and groaning as he came inside her body while Christopher's thick stiff cock pulsed and twitched between her lips, filling her mouth with salty, delicious juice.

After a moment she withdrew the wooden phallus very gently and pulled up her panties, then sat up, shaking a little, and went on with her work. She could feel her copious juices spreading on to the silky fabric of her panties. Well, she thought, if they smell me, I'll give them the right impression. I should start as I mean to go on.

The third man was more easy to categorise than Christopher had been. His name was Edmond and he had a fair, fine-featured, aristocratic face and bright, pale eyes. His hair was soft and a little longer than average and it flopped over his high brow in a Brideshead sort of way. In the photograph he was smiling rather lopsidedly: the expression brought out a deep dimple in his left cheek, irresistibly charming. He had met Kate with smooth, quiet courtesy, talking in a clipped, quick voice that betrayed his upper-class background and a public school education. It was interesting to read what his manager said about him: 'So polite that people walk over him. He can't get his own way; he can't get acceptance for his own ideas. As for criticising his staff, forget it: he'd think it was rude.'

Well, I can deal with that, thought Kate. She looked again at the photograph of Edmond. He looks sensitive, she thought, the type who really cares what a woman wants. I bet he's good with his tongue. The thought sent a little delicious shiver running through her.

She shifted the papers and revealed the face of the one female participant. Kate's mouth twitched uncomfortably. This could be the problem one, she knew. Men were susceptible to women, manageable, but if this girl, Sophie, decided that she wanted to dig in her heels and be awkward, she could ruin Kate's most interesting ideas.

She looked at the photograph with concentration. Sophie did not look like the sort of woman who would welcome a course based around sex: she looked passive and withdrawn. Her face was pretty, heart-shaped, with big dark eyes and a cloud of curly brown hair, but her expression was timid and frightened, as if she was afraid that the camera would bite her. Reading the notes Kate found that Sophie also tended to behave in a withdrawn way at work: her manager wrote, 'She is very intelligent indeed and has excellent ideas. However, it is always necessary to tease them out of her. I have never once heard her volunteer a suggestion or say that she wants something.' A male manager, Kate noticed.

Kate sat back, looking at Sophie's photograph and shaking her head. Why do so many women find it impossible to say what they want? Why are they forced into supportive roles, sidelined, passed over, because they cannot master the art of speaking their minds in a way that gets them listened to? She felt sorry for Sophie, a good brain and a pretty face trapped by unreasonable fear, but she was more worried about the success of her course. If Sophie turned out to be a prude it could ruin everything. Kate reminded herself that on this occasion the course was running not for the benefit of the participants but for her own pleasure. She decided coldly that if Sophie looked as if she would be a dampener on the proceedings she would deal with it at once by sending her away, saying she wasn't ready for the course yet. That would leave just three men and her. The thought filled her with delicious anticipation.

Her watch said five past six: time to go down and begin. She liked being a little late, it was guaranteed to draw attention to her. She tossed back her heavy hair and smiled at herself in the mirror, then went to the door.

As she had expected, the delegates were already in the bar waiting for her. Each of them had a glass and she quickly noticed what they were drinking. Edmond, Pimm's; Christopher, gin and tonic; Nick, a bottle of some expensive lager; Sophie, something that looked suspiciously like a mineral water. No surprises there. Edmond got up politely as she came into the bar and the other men looked shee-pish then did the same. They were all dressed quite formally, though not in suits. Edmond and Nick were both wearing jackets and ties, and Kate smiled to see that Edmond's tie was an old-school job, navy blue with some sort of crest, while Nick's was a loud affair that looked as if it might be by Moschino. Christopher wore a loose, well-cut turtle-neck shirt of knitted dark-grey cotton that showed off his muscular torso and gave him the look of a secret agent. Sophie had on an unobtrusive dress in a sort of drab olive colour, as if she wanted to vanish into the woodwork.

'Can I get you something?' Nick asked, just before Edmond. Kate smiled at him and said, 'No, no, there's a tab. Does anyone want anything else?' They all shook their heads: cautious, apprehensive and on their best behaviour, as participants always are at the beginning of a course. Kate went to the bar and ordered a spritzer made with dry wine and carried the glass back to the table.

The bar was quiet and unobtrusively opulent. Kate glanced around: nobody was within hearing distance of their table. 'Well,' she said brightly, 'since we're all here and there are no late arrivals, we might as well get started, if it's OK by all of you.'

They glanced at each other and Nick said cheerfully, 'Fire away, boss.'

'Not boss,' Kate said, pleased to have an opportunity to correct him at once. He was too cocky for his own good. She hoped the description was accurate in other ways as well. 'I don't tell you what to do. You're all here because you want to be.'

'I'm not,' said Nick, determined not to be put down. 'My boss sent me.'

The other participants exchanged uncomfortable glances: they had not expected direct confrontation so early on. Kate smiled a little, then asked patiently, 'Well, what do you think you're going to get out of this?'

'Bugger all,' Nick said curtly. 'Influencing? I reckon I'm already pretty influential.'

'So why didn't you persuade your boss that you didn't need to come?' asked Kate. She saw the faces of the other men move from her to Nick like spectators at Wimbledon, but Sophie was staring at her, her mouth a little open, looking astonished.

Nick hesitated. Then he said with a little more interest, 'What's persuasion got to do with it? I thought this was about getting your own way.'

'It is,' Kate grinned. 'But there's more than one way of getting your own way. If you're here and you don't want to be – then you didn't. Do you see what I mean?'

Nick's face darkened into a scowl. 'I suppose so,' he said with ill grace.

The other participants seemed to relax slightly and Kate smiled at them all. She said, 'Remember the definition of influence. You're influential when you succeed in changing someone's behaviour, but you maintain the relationship.' She looked around again at their earnest faces. 'Look, I don't want to get into details now, but I'll just set a few ground rules before we go on to the introductions; a course contract, if you like. Here's what you have to remember.' She sat up straight and used her hands for emphasis, her best model of an influential person. 'This course is a safe environment. Everything you say here is confidential, and I mean everything. Nothing goes back to your boss. I write a report on you, but it's depersonalised: it just says whether I think you put in sufficient effort, and whether I think you benefited from what I tried to show you.' She smiled into the eyes of each of them. They were gazing at her, deadly serious, and she felt a sudden rush of power. They were in her hands for the next four days. For a moment she imagined herself getting to her feet and unbuttoning her dress, revealing her body beneath it, and the four of them kneeling before her, entreating her like supplicants before a queen, stretching out their hands to beg her to be kind to them. The thought filled her with a rush of arousal and she licked her lips and swallowed hard.

'But I want you all to promise too,' she went on, 'that you won't divulge anything you learn about the other participants to anyone, anyone at all, without their permission.' She paused: there was silence. She sensed that Nick was waiting to be addressed, and purposefully looked at Edmond first. 'Edmond?'

'Well, yes. Of course.' His light voice was clipped and correct.

'Sophie?'

'Yes, I promise.'

'Nick?' She wasn't going to ask him last, either.

'Well, all right,' Nick said, still grudgingly. He was behaving childishly, but that was a typical reaction of an aggressive person who finds himself not in control.

'Christopher?'

'Wouldn't dream of it.'

'Good.' Kate sat back a little and allowed her gestures to expand. 'So as I said, this is a safe environment. Anything goes. You can practise what you like. Try things that might seem really way out in the office: you might be surprised by how effective they can be. I'm going to set the tone to start with, until you get used to what we're doing, but you have to feel free to disagree with me and make suggestions if there's something you would rather do. Try to influence me. Use your imaginations.'

'You'd be amazed what I can imagine,' Nick said boldly, and he laughed. Sophie and Edmond seemed unimpressed, but Christopher also laughed, a short, cynical laugh.

'You'd have to be quite creative to surprise me,

Nick,' Kate said coolly. She looked Nick in the face and raised one eyebrow and felt a sudden pulse pass between them, like an electric spark.

'That sounds like a challenge,' commented Christopher.

'Oh, it is,' Kate agreed. She took a sip of her drink. 'Now, how do we structure the course? Well, it's four days. We've split down the components of influence into three: bridging – that's finding out what others want; persuasion – that's convincing others to see your point of view; and assertion – that's making others understand your rights. Each day we'll do a little theory, then we'll practise one type of behaviour, then on day four we bring them all together. It's that simple. Lots of practice. Think about all the situations that you find difficult, and we'll practise them.'

'We were asked to bring difficult situations with us,' Sophie offered in her quiet voice. 'Things that we're really facing at the moment.'

'Quite right. It'll save you some time. But you may want to use different ones, too; I have some fairly unusual ideas for this course. I'm sure you'll all enjoy it, though.' They looked intrigued. Kate was going to say more, but one of the hotel staff came over and said, 'Excuse me, but your table is ready.'

'Over dinner,' Kate said as they sat down, 'I suggest we introduce each other. As you know, I'm Kate, from the Training and Development division. What I would like is for you to talk to your neighbour for the next five minutes or so and then tell us something about them. Not work, that's boring: about what they like to do when they're not at work.'

She sat quietly and watched for the next five minutes while the four of them tentatively began to talk. Christopher was talking to Nick and Edmond to Sophie. She was not surprised to see that Nick was monopolising his conversation, while Sophie and Edmond seemed to be doing fine, talking earnestly together in quiet voices.

'Christopher,' Kate said, 'would you like to start off?'

'Sure.' Christopher's voice was like his body, big but restrained, soft and dark-edged: a smoky voice. He looked almost shy, but something about his face made Kate think that it was not shyness that held him back. He gestured with one big hand at Nick.

'This is Nick. He's a busy boy, he works like a dog but he finds time for lots of other things. He plays squash and football at weekends. He likes fast cars, he came here in a Porsche, and from what he says he likes fast women too.' Christopher's voice was dry, revealing no approval. 'If you believe him he's slept with every woman in the office and several outside it.'

Nick smirked and Kate raised her eyebrows. 'I think I can disprove that for a start,' she said, and Nick's complacent expression was replaced by one of anger. 'Thanks, Christopher; an excellent thumbnail sketch. Nick, what did you find out about Christopher?'

Nick opened his mouth, then fell silent. After a second he said, 'Er, this is Christopher. He works in the computer consultancy division. Er, that's all I found out.'

Kate raised her brows. 'I said not to tell us about work.'

'Sorry,' Nick said, scowling at her.

'Well,' said Kate, 'never mind. Sophie, would you like to tell us about Edmond?'

'Edmond,' Sophie said in a voice that was instantly attractive, soft and sweet, 'seems to have a lovely life. He lives in the country in a small house with a big garden, there's a stream in the garden, and he spends a lot of time there reading and listening to music. And he goes to the theatre a lot when he's in London.' She glanced around at the others and added shyly, 'We discovered we like some of the same things.'

'Sophie likes plays and opera too,' Edmond volunteered, 'and she likes walking in the countryside, so we had a lot in common.' He smiled at Kate and she smiled back, delighted to see that Sophie obviously found Edmond attractive and that the feeling was mutual. If they were interested in each other perhaps Sophie would be easier to draw out of her shell. 'I like this way of introducing people,' Edmond went on. 'I should add that Sophie is an experienced sky-diver.'

'What?' demanded Nick, obviously astonished.

'A sky-diver. She's been doing it for years. I was very impressed.'

Nick grinned broadly at Sophie. 'Good God,' he said, 'I'd never have guessed it. What about it, Sophie, is it really better than sex?'

Sophie flushed scarlet and looked away. She did not reply and Nick immediately launched into an anecdote of a friend of his who had tried bungee jumping and had decided it was better than sex. He was monopolising the whole table, but the story was well told and entertaining and nobody seemed prepared to interrupt him.

Am I going to let him do this? Kate wondered. What shall I do? If I let him get away with it, will he ruin everything for the rest of the group by being so bloody cocky?

But he was so attractive. He had heavy eyelids and long, thick dark lashes over eyes that looked as if they were made out of the sky, a bright clear sky early on a summer morning, and his dark hair was fine and springy and strong. It was very carefully cut, Kate noticed, and she wouldn't be surprised to find a tub of Brylcreem on Nick's bathroom shelf: he didn't look like the sort of man who would spurn artificial aids.

She stopped herself from jumping as she felt a touch on her leg. For a moment she wondered who it was, then she saw by the gleam in Nick's bright eyes that it was him. She could feel his toes caressing her naked calf: he must have pushed off his shoes. He had been wearing deck shoes, she remembered, without any socks. The touch of his bare foot on her leg made her breathe quickly and deeply.

Nick went on telling his story. It really was funny: Sophie had overcome her embarrassment and was laughing and even Edmond and Christopher were beginning to pay attention. As Nick spoke his toes climbed up Kate's leg beneath her skirt, sliding gently over her skin. How often have you rehearsed telling that story, so you can do it without even thinking about it? Kate wondered. She could feel her nipples getting harder under her linen dress as Nick's foot advanced towards her crotch, and she let her thighs move apart.

The story ended and everybody laughed. Edmond said, 'That reminds me,' and Nick eased himself back in his chair and glanced over at Kate. His sleepy sensual eyes were very sharp under their lowered lids. His foot slipped between her thighs and very gently his toe slipped forward until it was resting on the crotch of her panties. He wriggled his toe experimentally and Kate suppressed a gasp. Nick caught his lower lip in his teeth and smiled as if in appreciation of Edmond's story and began very gently to rub his toe against Kate, massaging her engorged flesh through the tight fabric that covered it. She swallowed, trying to control her breathing. Her heavy hair was suddenly hot on the back of her neck. It was as if he could tell when his touch made her jump, made her buttocks clench with the sudden sharp pleasure of it. He put his toe on her clitoris and moved it, slowly, firmly, rubbing in little circles.

Kate could not stand it. If he went on she would come: her face and throat and shoulders would redden in a tell-tale flush and her breath would come fast and everybody would know. She pushed her chair back, pulling away from him, and said with a smile, 'Excuse me: shan't be a minute.' She headed towards the long corridor that led to the ladies', shaking her head and lifting her hair with her fingers.

The ladies' room was smart, large and thickly carpeted, with mirrors and heaps of towels and boxes of tissue and cotton wool on the tables. She sat down in front of the mirror and looked at herself, then went and splashed water on to her hot cheeks. 'That was close,' she said to herself in the mirror.

The door opened. Kate glanced up, then gasped: it was Nick, heading towards her. His lean jaw was set with determination. 'Nick!' Kate gasped. 'You can't come in here.'

'I'm in here, aren't I?' Nick retorted. 'And you're going to come in here, too, Kate.' He caught her by the arm and pulled her after him into the cubicle at the end of the row. 'You're off your head,' she hissed, but he slammed the door of the cubicle and turned on her.

'You looked at me,' he said. 'You wanted me. Why did you run away when we were just getting somewhere?'

'Because you look like the sort of cocky bastard who would take advantage if I let you,' she retorted angrily.

'My God, you were hot,' Nick said, coming towards her. 'The crotch of your panties was soaking. Anyone would think you'd already been fucked tonight. Let me feel.' Before Kate could tell him no he had caught her by her shoulders and was kissing her. His tongue was hot and hard, exploring her mouth, and she gasped and returned the kiss. Nick's mouth tasted of wine, sweet and sharp.

He pressed her against the wall of the cubicle and scowled in concentration as he struggled with the buttons on her dress. At last it was undone to the waist and he pulled it apart to reveal her lacy bra. Without a word he pushed his hand inside the bra, cupping her breast, catching her nipple between his fingers and squeezing it hard. Exquisite pleasure flooded through her. The breath left her body all at once and she caught his head in her hands and pulled his mouth down on to hers harder. She knew that she should turn him down, refuse him; he was unbearable enough as it was; if she let him have her it would only make things worse. But she wanted him so much. She could feel his thickening penis inside his trousers, pulsing and hot, trembling in its eagerness to have her, and she could not resist it. She wanted him as much as he wanted her.

They heard the door of the ladies' open and both of them pulled back and froze, looking anxiously towards the door of the cubicle. Footsteps crossed the floor and entered the cubicle next door; they heard the rustle of clothes and the tinkle of urine. A lazy smile crossed Nick's face; he leant forward and kissed Kate again, slowly and lasciviously, still squeezing her breast with one hand, while with the other he continued to unbutton her dress. The woman beside them sighed, flushed the loo and left the cubicle as Nick's hand slipped through Kate's skirt and ran across her thighs. Nick smiled wickedly, then lifted her panties and eased one finger inside.

'Wet,' he whispered into her ear, 'dripping wet.' His finger slid across the moist lips of her sex, stroking gently along their length, and ended up at the front, just below her dark triangle of pubic hair, caressing and stimulating the little point that was the centre of her desire. Hot arrows of sensation pierced her and her legs felt weak and shaky: she smothered a moan of need.

The door closed again. 'Oh God,' Kate burst out, 'do it, Nick.' As he dragged down his tie and pulled his collar open she fumbled for his fly and unzipped it and thrust her hand inside, feeling for his cock. There it was, hot and hard beneath her fingers, a magnificent column of flesh. She pulled herself free of his mouth and looked down at the glorious disarray: her dress half open and rucked off her shoulder, one breast bare and clutched in Nick's working hand, her skirt unbuttoned and her thighs spread apart and her panties pushed down to allow his finger deep into her aching sex, Nick's tie awry and his trousers open and his gorgeous thick hard cock held quivering and ready in her hand. She felt so aroused she could barely stand.

'Now,' she said. Nick bent quickly and stripped her panties down her legs. She stepped out of them and he moved up between her thighs, pressing her hard against the cold tiled wall. There were no preliminaries: he felt for the wet swollen lips of her sex, fitted the hot smooth head of his cock between them, drew his lips back from his teeth in a snarl of pleasure and thrust.

'Oh God,' Kate whimpered, feeling the hot dry shaft entering her, 'God.' Nick groaned as the whole of him slid into her. He took hold of her breasts and squeezed the nipples harder and harder and buried his head in Kate's shoulder as he thrust and withdrew. She put her hands on his buttocks, feeling the muscles there clenching and relaxing, driving in and out of her. Simple, direct, crude sex: it was so good. He moved slowly, pushing in deeply, the hairy root of his cock rubbing hard against her shivering clitoris with every thrust, and as he pinched her nipples and bit her shoulder she felt herself beginning to come. Her head rolled helplessly and she moaned and Nick lifted his head and put his mouth on hers to keep her quiet and forced himself further and further into her and she began to convulse, her tongue quivering in her mouth, her hips jerking helplessly towards him.

'That's it,' Nick whispered into her open lips. 'That's it. Come on, come on. Feel me. I want to feel you come.'

Kate threw back her head and it cracked against the wall of the cubicle. She didn't care: her orgasm was sweeping over her, filling her with glorious, shuddering pleasure. Nick gasped and bit her throat. He began to move faster and she clutched tighter at his wonderful round arse as he plunged in and out. Every thrust was bliss, her climax seemed to go on for ever. He gripped her breasts tightly, her stiff nipples trapped between his strong fingers, and drove his stiff shaft into her as if he wanted to nail her to the wall. 'God,' he whispered, 'I'm coming, I'm coming.' He gave a long choked moan and closed his eyes and she felt him shuddering as he gave a final convulsive heave and his own orgasm gripped him.

They stood still, panting. Nick let his head fall on to her throat and she stroked his silky hair, feeling his penis stirring faintly as it lay deeply imbedded in her moist flesh. Then they jumped: a timid tap sounded on the door of the cubicle and a middle-aged voice said hesitantly, 'Are you all right, my dear?'

Kate tried not to laugh. 'I'm fine,' she called. 'Sorry for the noises: touch of constipation. I'll get something for it from the desk in a little while.'

'You poor thing,' said the voice. 'I'm a martyr to it myself. Can I fetch you anything?'

Nick was laughing, smothering the sound against

Kate's shoulder. 'It's all right,' Kate called. 'I'll be fine. Thank you for asking.'

'That's all right, dear,' said the voice. The door opened and closed and Nick let out a great gust of laughter; he nearly fell over. 'Persuasiveness!' he said, gently withdrawing from Kate. 'You think fast, I'll give you that.'

'Never lose your cool,' said Kate sententiously.

'Perhaps there is something I can learn from you.' Nick stretched and pushed his hands through his hair.

'Why, what would you have said?' asked Kate as she wiped herself and began to fasten her dress.

'I'd have told her to fuck off and mind her own business,' Nick said, zipping up his trousers. He cocked his head and admitted with a wry smile, 'It might not have been so effective.'

Kate smiled at him, then stooped to retrieve her panties. 'There you are,' she said. 'There'll be more like that, I promise. Will you be a good boy, Nick?'

'As long as you deliver,' Nick said. He was still smiling, but there was a challenge in his eyes. Without waiting for an answer he opened the door of the cubicle and darted out. Kate saw him stick his head out of the door, look both ways, then saunter off as if nothing had happened. She looked down at herself: yes, flushed from throat to breasts. Oh well, she thought, it was bound to happen. Might as well start as I mean to go on.

The Gilded Cage

Juliet Hastings

The Gilded Cage

Helena Dalassena, at Constantinople, to her daughter Eirene in Antioch, greeting.

It is strange, my daughter, that when you lived at home we hardly knew each other, and since you have gone so far away we have become close. And yet, as you will see, there is still much concerning me that you do not know.

You tell me in your latest letter that you are in love with a man not your husband, a young Frankish knight. Let me see, what did you say? You described his charms and your mutual passion in words that made me shiver, and then you ended: *I could not resist him, I wanted him so much. I do not expect you to understand, mother.*

But I do understand, Eirene. You will see that I am writing this letter with my own hand, because now I will tell you something of my past, something that I have never revealed to anyone. And when you have read this letter, you will know why it is that I understand, and why I do not condemn you for what you have done.

As you know, my daughter, my first husband died when I was twenty four and still childless. Two years later I lived at the court of the Emperor Alexius Comnenus, one of the noblewomen in attendance on his daughter, the Princess Anna Comnena.

Anna was proud and haughty. She favoured early rising and fixed hours for communal prayer. Her shrewd eyes were always watching, alert for any impropriety, and she remembered everything. Everything!

The Princess was not pretty. Intelligent, yes. Well attired, of course, in the finest silk embroidered with gems, her black hair braided with pearls and her diadem studded with emeralds. But definitely not attractive to men, who found her quick, almost masculine appraisal of their character and abilities more disquieting than appealing.

On the other hand, men admired me. I was as lovely then as you are now, Eirene. Courtiers compared my skin to molten honey, my eyes to a fawn's, my nipples to the buds of a scarlet rose. Some said that I must have been named after the fabulous Helen of Troy. So you can imagine that our plain Princess detested me most cordially.

Sexual activity was frowned on in the Palace, and I always avoided drawing attention to myself. But when we went to our country villas to escape the hot weather, things were different. Do I shock you yet, daughter? If so, put this letter down, for my language will become stronger, much stronger.

I had a lover who was perfection. Tender, cultured, and marvellously inventive in the ritual of the bed. His caresses were sensual, subtle, exquisite, the peak of erotic artistry. Long sensitive fingers, tipped with hard white nails, touched me with such delicacy that every inch of my skin yearned for more. Our love play was so languid, so luxurious that it outlasted our lamp, and when at last he entered me I moaned with the rapture of climax, hardly feeling him moving within me, hardly hearing his gasp as his seed pulsed forth.

Yes, your father Michael was perfection. But he was also a general in the Emperor's army, and at the time of which I write he was gone, ridden to the East to help secure the tottering borders of the Empire against the encroaching Scythians. I yearned for his return and hoped in secret that when he came back we might marry. But marriages are made by diplomacy, not by affection, and the brilliant, brittle Court was no place to display my longings.

Each day that passed I missed his company, and each night as I lay in the Princess' chamber I wished for his warm, hard body, for his inquisitive hands. In the darkness I touched myself, remembering what he had done to me. His questing tongue, warm and moist, soft and hard together, flicking at the points of my breasts until they ached, tracing lines of chilly bliss on the insides of my thighs, lapping, lapping against that enchanted spot, stimulating me with such agonising gentleness that I could not make a sound until my final, helpless cry of anguish and ecstasy.

In June I would go to my villa, and then I might

find a replacement. It was April now, and I knew I must wait. To do otherwise would be to risk the Princess' anger. I was not daring enough to emulate the Palace women who met their lovers in the sweet-smelling labyrinth of the gardens, baring their white breasts to the cool air, opening their thighs beneath the shelter of an overhanging rose. Or those who took rougher pleasure within the Palace, with a servant perhaps, or one of the Emperor's personal bodyguard. Did any of your Palace friends ever have a Varangian guardsman as her lover, Eirene? My friends favoured those big blond warriors from the cold North and whispered that under their mail shirts they carried fleshy weapons fit to match their four-foot axes. But I have never been attracted to blond men. And besides, to allow a Varangian between your legs was to expose yourself to blackmail, and to disgrace and punishment, if it were ever discovered. It was not in my nature to take such risks.

But then the Crusaders came.

We had expected their arrival for months. They came, they said, to free the Holy Places of Palestine from the hand of Islam: but the Emperor Alexius expected them to take a bite out of his Empire along the way, if they were not cleverly handled. So when they arrived at Constantinople the rabble were kept outside the city and the lords housed at once in palaces within the walls, under careful military surveillance.

Most of all the Emperor feared the Norman adventurer Bohemond of Taranto. Yes, Eirene, that same Bohemond who now rules your city of Antioch and is dignified with the title of Prince. You know that the Normans are a formidable race, clever, wily, ambitious and ruthless, and their men are the fiercest, most committed fighters you can meet. The Court assembled to receive this barbarian war-leader with a mixture of anticipation and apprehension.

We were dressed with particular care, draped with silk and glittering with jewels. The Princess was so bedecked that she resembled an animated doll made all of gold and precious stones. The hall of audience was hung with purple, and beside the inlaid Imperial throne stood a silver cage full of marvellous mechanical birds that sang as if they were alive. The Varagians lined the walls, holding their axes at parade rest. We meant to awe these Norman brutes into respect for us.

Alas, we failed. Bohemond and his men marched into the hall with barely a glance around them, as determined to be unimpressed as we were to impress them.

I stood behind the Princess, avidly examining these Western adventurers. They had only just arrived, and their faces were weary and their clothes still travel-stained. They smelled of horses and male sweat, and I could not restrain a little sussuration of disgust.

They were clean shaven for the most part and wore their hair short. This made them look like boys beside a roomful of bearded Byzantines – until I saw their eyes. Then I knew why they were feared wherever they carried their long swords.

Bohemond was tall, blond, perfectly proportioned, formidable. He prepared to kneel to the Emperor, and I thought that everyone would be watching. It would be safe now to look into their faces, with no risk of meeting those dangerous eyes. But I was wrong. Just behind Bohemond stood his *aide-de-camp*, and as I looked at him, so he looked directly at me.

His gaze made me flinch as if he had struck me. Never had I seen eyes like his, bluer than borage flowers, brilliant as sapphires. They showed all the more brightly because his skin was quite pale and his lashes were long and dark. Hair the colour of a ripe chestnut sprang from his high brow in unruly waves and was cropped short on the nape of his neck. His features were bony and strong and his lips had a sensual curve that stopped my heart. It was hard to guess his age, but I thought he was younger than Bohemond, in his early thirties perhaps. He stood with casual, graceful ease, like a powerful animal, and he was tall and broad shouldered and carried the weight of his heavy mail shirt without effort.

Never have I seen a man so striking. I remember vividly how I felt when I first saw him. I believed that his people were ruffians, thieves of land and gold, rapists, murderers, separated from the beasts only by low cunning. So I shivered and was afraid of him, because I could not understand how such wickedness could coexist with such beauty. I felt as a tame bird must feel when a cat sits by its gilded cage and bares its teeth.

My heart pounded and my breath came quickly. He must have read my face, for as I stared his brilliant eyes narrowed and the pupils opened, darkening his gaze with a shadow of lust. He smiled very slightly and lifted his hand to his mouth.

I thought that he meant to blow me a kiss, as a courtier might. No, no. His hand was big, with dirty broken nails, as unlike Michael's as could be imagined. He clenched it into a fist. I gazed, mesmerised. His strong pale wrist was circled with a broad band of barbaric gold. As I wondered what it would be like to feel that hand roughened with toil and travel moving over my tender skin, he took his thumb in his mouth like a child and sucked it, then withdrew it from his lips, wet and shining. He thrust it into his closed fist. The broad ball of it appeared between his index and middle fingers, scarlet and glistening, and he moved it slowly back and forth in an obscene, lewd, unmistakable gesture.

Blood rushed to my cheeks. I gasped, smothered the sound lest the Princess hear me, and jerked my eyes away.

My pulse pounded in my ears and I could not keep my breathing steady. I was disgusted, appalled. But his action had filled my mind with sexual images, flashes that were half memory, half fantasy. A man's naked penis, erect and shining and ready for love, its bulging glans gleaming like the wet tip of his thumb. A man's hands gripping at the soft swell of a woman's buttocks, parting them, the head of his swollen phallus nudging between the soft spheres. A woman's throat arched in ecstasy. And above all, the image of a man's hard flesh opening a woman's sex, penetrating her, sliding into her deeper, deeper. I fought the images and the words too, words that I knew I should not articualte even in my mind. But they surged up, unstoppable. Hold me. Take me. Put your cock inside me.

This was not the delicate ritual of the Court, the leisurely, exquisite erotic encounter. This was something more elemental, more brutal. It horrified me even as it thrilled me. How could he have put such thoughts into my mind just with a gesture?

Unable to help myself, I glanced at him again. He was watching me, his face still and intent. When he saw me look his way his eyes glittered and those sensual lips curved in a smile of – of what? Contempt, admiration, amusement? He raised his straight brows quizzically and my fading blush surged again to my cheeks. I fastened my gaze on a jewel at the back of the Princess' diadem, determined not to look at him any more.

It seemed an eternity before the audience ended, but at last the Normans were escorted away to their palace and we were allowed to retire. Anna spent some time fulminating against Bohemond. I listened to her with barely concealed disdain. I knew that the vehemence of her professed dislike only reflected the vehemence of the physical attraction she felt for that barbarian chieftain.

Presently the Princess went to discuss politics with her father the Emperor. We women were bored with politics, and we remained in our chambers to discuss that much more interesting subject, the men.

One of our number, Zoe, held us spellbound. 'Imagine,' she whispered, clutching her arms across her breasts, 'imagine taking such an animal to your bed!'

She spoke of Bohemond, but it was not Bohemond that I imagined.

'Imagine how he would bite you! Claw you! Take you like a brute!'

I could feel already his hard hands pinning down my arms, his dirty nails scoring red weals on my tender breasts, his powerful body pounding into mine, fierce and relentless.

'Perhaps,' suggested Zoe, leaning forward and practically crowing with delight, 'perhaps he would take you on all fours, from behind. Perhaps he would grip your neck between his teeth, like a mating leopard.'

His breath was hot on my nape. His strong white teeth dented my skin, holding me still to receive his surging thrusts. I cried out in desperate surrender as his thick phallus plunged inside my sheath, driving me into delirium and ecstasy.

'Perhaps,' Zoe's voice rose to a squeak of excitement, 'perhaps he would be hung like a stallion, too!'

'What is this – depravity?' enquired a cold, composed voice at the door.

It was the Princess, white with anger. We drew apart, bowing low. I hung my head, knowing that my cheeks were flushed with desire.

Anna moved slowly between us, looking at each face. 'You dare to – speculate – on the attractions of these barbarians?' Her voice was icy. 'To imagine how they might – serve you?' She stopped before poor trembling Zoe and waited, patient as a lurking spider.

'My lady – '

Anna struck Zoe sharply around the face. Then

she turned and raked us all with her black eyes. 'I know that some of you find – amusement about the Court,' she hissed, 'despite all I have done to extirpate such lewdness. But believe me, ladies,' and she imbued the word 'ladies' with unutterable scorn, 'that if I discover that any of you has allowed one of these barbarous foreigners so much as to kiss her hand I will have her whipped. And for a worse misdemeanour, by Heaven, there will be a worse penalty.'

I am not a bold woman, as you know, my daughter. I am not a risk-taker. But now I was filled with resentment. She desired Bohemond herself! She was a hypocrite! I wished I had smiled back at that blue-eyed Norman reprobate, licked my lips and fluttered my eyelashes and done everything that a woman can to express interest.

But I had not. And now, of course, it was too late.

I thought of him as I lay in my bed, and then I felt guilty and forced myself to think of Michael. But when I fell asleep my body ruled my brain.

I dreamed. I was with Michael in his summer palace, naked in his naked arms. We kissed and touched, drawing ourselves into that state of heightened arousal from which the only thing that can proceed is penetration. He lay back and I straddled him and lowered myself on to his erect penis, sighing with bliss as I allowed him to impale me. He took hold of my breasts and stroked my nipples as I slid up and down, up and down on his slippery shaft.

Then suddenly his face changed from pleasure to fear. Someone was behind me, a looming presence.

I tried to turn, but before I could free myself from Michael there was a hand on my neck, pressing me down until my face was against Michael's, my mouth on his, both of us moaning in protest.

And then I felt another man's body between my open thighs. The head of a hot, stiff cock nudged at that place where Michael's penis was embedded in my snug, moist sheath. Michael's eyes opened wide as he felt it too, pressing against his buried shaft, sliding along it.

He meant to put himself within me at the same time as Michael. It was not possible, it would split me open! And yet as the smooth head prodded and thrust I whimpered – not with pain and fear but with appalled, unbelieving ecstasy, and Michael moaned too as he felt another cock sliding into me to lie beside him, rubbing against the sensitive underside of his hidden penis.

The intruding presence began to move to and fro, gliding in and out of my wide-stretched sex, pleasuring Michael as it pleasured me. My lover's hands tightened on my aching nipples and his tongue slid deep into my gasping mouth. We lay motionless as the powerful virile creature behind me ravished us both, bringing us to helpless ecstasy with the strong strokes of his thick shaft. I climaxed first, trapped between two hot male bodies and twisting with rapture as Michael's tongue coiled within my mouth and the stranger's cock drove into my spasming sex. Then Michael groaned and clutched at me and shuddered as he came. And at last the shadow snarled like an animal and seized Michael's tense buttocks and pulled him close, crushing me between them as his huge penis throbbed and jerked within my very womb.

For several nights I had similar dreams, full of darkenss and smothered violence. Sometimes those blue eyes were in my dream, but more often it was just a faceless shadow. But I knew, when I woke moist and trembling, who had made my secret flesh silky and swollen with longing.

The Emperor intended the Normans to travel immediately across the Bosphorus and cease to threaten us. I knew I should be glad. How could a noblewoman of the Byzantine Empire seek a liaison with a warrior from the remote West, a freebooter, a brigand? Why should I care whether he lived or died?

Because I was obsessed. Do you remember, Eirene, how when you were thirteen you doted upon that Hippodrome chariot-driver? You pinned his colours to your undergown, screamed when he lost, fainted when he won, felt sick when he walked past your window. I was twice thirteen years old, but just as smitten. I hid behind pillars to gaze surreptitiously at Bohemond's *aide-de-camp*. I discovered his name: Adhemar.

Adhemar. A barbarous name, hard to pronounce, harder to write. I murmured it as I fell asleep, whispered it on waking. I remembered his brilliant eyes, his lazy smile over his clenched, obscene fist. Possessed by recklessness, I wrote on a slip of parchment: Meet me tomorrow in the imperial box of the Hippodrome, at noon. I wrote it in Latin and in the Latin character, using large, simple letters, hoping that he was less illiterate than his countrymen.

Then I looked at the note and shook my head. I was about to screw it up and fling it away, but something stopped me. At last I folded it and tucked it carefully into the bosom of my gown, beneath my jewelled belt. I had no intention of sending it. After all, whom could I trust to take it? Every servant and slave in the Court was an imperial spy. Anna would have me whipped, have my head shaved, send me to a convent if she discovered it.

But the next day I heard that the Normans were with the Emperor, discussing final plans for the Crusade. They were to be ferried over the Bosphorus in three days' time. When I heard this I felt sick and empty, and within my sex a wrench of longing hurt me with dull immediacy, like the pain of my moon-blood.

I could not let him go without attempting to assuage the irrational craving that threatened to overwhelm me. I stood outside the Council chamber, shaking. When the doors opened at last and the Normans emerged I watched for him. I knew he would notice me.

He was there, walking behind his lord. His sharp blue eyes fixed on me and brightened as he began to smile. Then his face changed as I drew out the slip of paper from my gown and placed it on the base of a pillar at my right hand. I touched my finger to my lips and fled.

I did not know whether he picked it up, I did not dare even to turn back. I had put myself in his power, and at once I regretted it bitterly. Why had

I trusted him? He might ask a courtier to read it for him, might say, 'The Princess' woman left it, the pretty one.' He might tell all his friends. Worst of all, he might laugh and ignore it.

All night I tossed and turned, until the Princess' body-slave asked me if I had a fever. I told her yes without a lie, for I was flushed and sweating. So the next day I was excused Court duties and told to take the air.

It was as if fate intended me to keep my rendez-vous. I left the Palace in a litter, attended by a single slave, and jolted through the crowded streets between the lines of marble statues. Each heroic naked male body reminded me of my madness and my desire. When we came to the Hippodrome I called out, 'Stop!'

My companion looked at me, puzzled. I said, 'I am feeling unwell. Take me up to the Emperor's box.'

In the box I stretched myself out on the red silk couch. 'That is better,' I murmured. 'Now, I meant to deliver this message to my noble friend Antonia. You shall take it. When you return, wait with the litter below.'

After a little argument she went, and I was left alone. I sat up, shivering.

Noon was past. Had he been and gone, given up hope? Was he even now telling his friends that Byzantine women were professional teases? Did he hate me?

Silence. I went to the front of the box, rested my arms on the stone parapet and sighed as I stared out over the huge, empty, sun-drenched Hippodrome.

Empty? No. Beneath me was a single figure, moving slowly between the rows of stepped stone seats. I frowned, blinking in the brightness, and the figure turned and looked up at me.

It was Adhemar. He saw me above him and his blue eyes opened wide, then turned quite black as his pupils dilated. He ran towards me, leaping three steps at a time, faster than a pouncing lion. I gasped and reeled back into the dark shadows of the imperial box.

I could hear his swift footfalls and his sword jingling at his side. His steps came closer, closer, and then, suddenly, a pair of strong hands gripped the parapet. My dream became reality and became a nightmare. I was terrified. The door of the cage was open, the beast was approaching.

Smoothly, swiftly, as if it were easy, he pulled himself up onto the parapet, knelt there a moment, then jumped down inside the box. He was breathing quickly through open lips. I could see his white teeth and his fierce eyes. He took one step towards me and I gave a smothered cry and turned to flee.

Before I could reach the door his hands were on me. I tried to prise his fingers from my robe, but he grappled with me, forced me to turn and face him. Both of us were panting now. His breath was hot as his glowing eyes. He dragged my veil from my hair and thrust his face towards me and I writhed desperately, turning my mouth from his searching lips.

He clutched me close against him, wrenched back my head and buried his face against my throat. I thought he would bite me like the beast he was. I opened my mouth to scream.

But he pressed his parted lips to my tender skin and breathed, breathed again, long sobbing gasps. It was as if he wanted to inhale my very essence. My scream faded in my throat and I stood still. I was trembling from head to foot, but as his mouth stirred against me and his long eyelashes brushed my skin I realised that he was shaking too, hands, lips, body.

He murmured something, the words lost against my throat. Then, without warning, he sank to his knees. His arms encircled me, warm and strong, and he pressed his face against my breasts. I looked down at him, astonished. His eyes were closed and he kissed my body fervently through my silk garments, whispering, *'ma déesse, mon seul désir.'*

My goddess, my only desire. I knew enough to understand him. My fear began to leave me, displaced by my yearning. I put my hands in his hair and felt its softness. He glanced up at me, his eyes like stars. Then he set his lips to the point of my breast and sucked gently.

I let out a cry of urgent longing and held his head against me. My nipple stiffened and he smiled and set his teeth to the proud flesh through the silk. One of his hands reached down to my ankles, stole beneath my drapery, and began to slide gently up my leg.

My knees were weak with wanting him. I was about to drop down beside him and pull his mouth onto mine when I heard a sound outside the box.

Instantly I pulled away from him, panic-stricken. He tried to catch me back and I fought him off with such determination that he must have thought I had gone mad. He jumped to his feet, opening his mouth to protest. I pressed my hand over his lips and towed him to the curtained alcove in the corner where the cushions were kept.

We fell behind the curtain just as the door opened. I kept my hand over his mouth and signalled him desperately to be silent. If they found us here what would become of us?

The visitors were a party of country nobles, being shown the sights by some Court relative. They stood in the box, marvelling and chattering. I was limp with terror.

Adhemar's brilliant eyes crinkled at me and behind my hand his lips tightened into a smile. I shook my head earnestly. His gaze darkened and I jumped as I felt his tongue on my palm.

He explored the soft centre of my hand, caressing it with tongue and lips. I shuddered, as stirred as if he searched my secret flesh. He caught me by my buttocks and pulled me close to him. Beneath his clothes his penis was hot and hard, quivering with readiness. His tongue continued to slither against my silencing palm and he pushed his hips against me, grinding that thick rod of flesh against my mound. I bit my lip to stop myself from crying out and suddenly he jerked my hand from his face, pressed his lips against mine and thrust his tongue into my mouth.

I struggled, but Adhemar forced me back against the wall, trapping me. His hands reached for my aching breasts and his lips crushed mine. My resistance crumbled before his passion and I submitted to ecstasy. We kissed wildly, mouths gaping open, tongues searching.

The door of the box slammed shut. Adhemar

pulled away and threw back the curtain, laughing. He tugged me towards the Emperor's couch.

I laughed too. Desire and relief had burned away all my fear. I flung myself down beside him, lifted his tunic and took his penis in my hand, relishing its silken rigidity. He seemed startled, as if he were not accustomed to a woman taking the initiative. What other delights of Byzantine love might be strange to him? Gasping with excitement, I lowered my head and flicked my tongue quickly across the smooth shining tip of his cock.

He cried out in shock and astonishment. A shiver of incredulous wonder passed through me. So strong a warrior, and I was the first woman to offer him this! I moistened my lips slowly, savouring the moment, and then I took him into my mouth.

'*Face de Dieu*,' Adhemar moaned. His lean hips twisted up from the couch, seeking the soft depths of my throat. I sucked at him greedily, relishing the hot salty taste of man. My hands cradled the tight sac of his testicles, caressed the skin of his strong thighs, circled the base of his penis as my wet lips slid smoothly up and down his gleaming shaft. I sensed his tremendous excitement, his unstoppable eagerness, and I shuddered with the knowledge of my power over him.

His hands gripped like claws in my hair and his buttocks tightened as he thrust himself harder and harder into my mouth. I took him willingly, whimpering with delight as he penetrated my quivering lips. He began to gasp and shake. I wanted him to know the extremity of pleasure, and as I sucked I slid one finger between his clenched cheeks and eased it gently into his anus.

He cried out and his strong body arced upwards, rigid and taut. His nails dug into my scalp even as his cock pulsed and exploded within my mouth. I held myself still, swallowing as gently as I could, and then licked him clean like a cat.

After a few moments he sat up, shaking his head as if he had been knocked half unconscious. He looked down at his body as if he expected to find himself damaged in some way. I smiled and fondled his softened penis, showing him that all was well.

He said something more which I could not understand. Then he caught me by the shoulders and laid me on the couch. He fumbled for a moment with my complex robes, and I pushed his hands gently away and unfastened a brooch here, a button there, until he could part the layers of shimmering silk and expose my naked breasts.

With a sigh he bent his head to caress my nipples with his mouth, lapping and sucking at them in turn until I felt as if my breasts were tipped with burning ice. I was aroused beyond sense, writhing with need and the desire to feel his body within me. I dragged up my drapery around my hips and opened my thighs for him, offering him my body with eager shamelessness.

For a moment he was silent and still. Then he laid his big hand softly on the pale inside of my thigh. I shuddered. His skin was hard and the rough edges of his nails left infinitesimal scratches in my flesh. I closed my eyes. All my sensation was concentrated in the touch of his hand. Nothing else existed. I was a star of bliss in a sky of darkness, an island of ecstasy surrounded by a roaring ocean of danger.

His hand moved upwards, slowly, seeking out my heart. The rough pads of his fingers brushed my crisp fur, then stroked along my labia. I moaned. Gently, so gently, he parted the moist petals of my body's flower. He approached me humbly, timidly, as a sinner might approach the altar of forgiveness. His middle finger eased delicately into the centre of me and I moaned with involuntary excitement and clutched at him. Then, when I was penetrated, he touched me with his thumb, with the broad ball of that thumb which had first so aroused me. He touched me where I yearned and ached to be touched, and as he touched me I climaxed.

He held me, caressing me gently until my spasms subsided. He was trembling. When I was still, he moved up between my open legs and the head of his penis pressed into me. He stopped there, looking down into my eyes. For a moment I did not understand what he wanted. Then I knew. I reached up and took his head in my hands and lifted my mouth to his. As my tongue signalled my willingness he slowly slid his long, thick cock into me, filling me.

His eyes were wide open, awestruck. At first he was as gentle as only a strong man can be, cradling me in his hands like a fragile flower, moving as if he thought I would break. But as our pleasure increased he began to reveal his power. His thrusts were not fast, but so long and deep that I groaned as he reached my womb. Slowly, strongly, he drove his body into mine. Sweat beaded on his high brow and above his sensual lips. His face showed wonder and delight.

Another climax hovered tensely in my heavy limbs. I cried out and offered my breasts to his hot mouth and lifted my sex towards his surging phallus. He bared his gritted teeth and pressed his body down on mine.

I did not want him to stop, and he did not. The speed of his thrusts increased until his hips were beating against mine as if he wanted to split me apart. I was consumed by him as if by a flame. He possessed me utterly. Everything that I was, was his.

Such ecstasy could not last. I arched against him as the strong fist of climax clutched my body. My sex pulsed around him and he groaned and fastened his lips to mine as his penis throbbed and jerked within me.

We lay very still for some minutes. Then he began, very gently, to stroke my face. I clung to him, trembling as I confronted the reality of my inevitable loss.

At last I disengaged myself and sat up, mumbling in Greek, 'I must go, they will be suspicious.'

He did not understand me. He stood up and watched me setting my clothes to rights, fastening my brooches, adjusting my hair. He picked up my veil and handed it to me. His eyes never left me.

When I was dressed he caught hold of my hand. He frowned as if he were concentrating. Then he said very carefully, in fairly correct Latin, 'When I have my fiefdom in Palestine, shall I send for you?'

I could not reply. All my energy was gone, my courage exhausted. I stared at him wide-eyed, then turned helplessly away. The cage was closed again.

He kissed my hand. Then he took off his heavy

gold bracelet, closed it around my naked wrist, and pulled down my sleeve to conceal it. I lifted my weighted hand to my face, hiding myself from the intensity of his eyes. When I raised my head he was gone.

You see, daughter, that I understand you better than you could have dreamed. I wish you joy of your lover, Eirene. I did not dare to follow the urging of my heart, and now I hope that you will have the courage to do all that you desire.

I know you will ask me what became of Adhemar. I cannot tell you. I never saw him or heard of him again. Perhaps he achieved his fiefdom and lives still in Palestine, a lord of men. Perhaps he died at the gates of Jerusalem. I will never know. Later that same year your father Michael returned from the East and secured my hand, and I put Adhemar from my mind.

But sometimes I wonder. If he had sent for me, could the bird have left the cage?

Cassandra's Conflict

Fredrica Alleyn

An anthology of Black Lace material has to include an extract from *Cassandra's Conflict*. This was one of the four titles which launched the series in July 1993 and is an archytypal Black Lace book in terms of cover picture and story content. In many ways, *Cassandra's Conflict* went on to set the tone for other erotic novels. This has been our best-selling title in the whole series.

Cassandra has broken up with her dull boyfriend and is changing the course of her life by applying for a job as a nanny in a house in Hampstead. But the image of cultural respectability is a facade for world of decadent indulgence and darkly bizarre eroticism. Her new employer – the Baron von Ritter – tests Cassandra to her sexual limits in games where only he knows the rules.

Fredrica Alleyn's success with *Cassandra's Conflict* encouraged her to write five other books for Black Lace. They are: *Fiona's Fate*, *Deborah's Discovery*, *Cassandra's Chateau* (the sequel to *Cassandra's Conflict*) and *Dark Obsession*. *The Bracelet*, Fredrica's sixth book in the series, is due for publication in September 1996.

Cassandra's Conflict

Cassandra was both excited and nervous as she watched the young driver take her two shabby suitcases out of the boot of the sleek black Daimler and carry them in through the front door of the baron's house. It was wonderful to feel needed, to know that someone actually wanted her to work for them, but it was also frightening to cut herself off from everything that she'd ever known before. She knew it was ridiculous, but in some ways this house in Hampstead seemed like a foreign country, and she had never had the courage to travel abroad.

At last she took a deep breath and followed Peter inside. There was no one in the hall. Her two cases had vanished; she assumed they'd been taken upstairs, and once again everywhere was silent. After a few seconds she heard light footsteps on the upstairs landing, and briefly remembered the strange cry that had come from that direction just as she was leaving after the interview. At the time she'd thought it was one of the children, but later, with time for her imagination to run riot, she'd convinced herself it was more like an adult's cry of pain and the thought had worried away at her like an intermittent toothache.

'I thought I heard the car!' a woman's voice exclaimed, and Cassandra looked up to see a young woman with a mass of silver-blonde hair that fell to her shoulders in a cascade of curls, coming down the stairs.

She was tiny, only a little over five feet tall, with delicate bones and her face glowed with a golden tan which accentuated her startling green eyes. To Cassandra she was like some wonderful exotic bird and the clinging minidress that she wore outlined the kind of figure that usually indicated hours of aerobics and swimming and a dedication to perfection that Cassandra always found unbelievable when she read about it in papers or magazines. However, looking at this young woman and guessing that she was the baron's fiancée, she couldn't help but realise that for women with enough time and money it undoubtedly made sense. A man like Baron von Ritter would only be drawn to beautiful things, and this young woman was definitely beautiful. It was the first time Cassandra had ever studied another woman's body so objectively, and as she realised what she was doing she quickly averted her eyes as she felt a blush spreading up her neck.

Katya had spent a considerable amount of time that morning getting ready for her meeting with this woman who, without knowing it, was her adversary in the game that was about to begin, and she felt a glow of satisfaction as she saw Cassandra's blush. She smoothed her hands down over her hips, as though straightening out some invisible wrinkles in the dress but actually emphasising her curves, and then held out her right hand in greeting.

'You must be Cassandra Williams. I'm Katya Guez, I live here with the baron and his adorable little daughters. They're such fun, but far too energetic for me I'm afraid. I'm a night owl, and they're a couple of larks. Now that you're here at least I'll get my beauty sleep again!'

She gave a girlish giggle, and Cassandra smiled back, totally unaware that Katya had never got out of her bed to see to either of the girls in her life, and that if she had her way they'd both be sent off to boarding school as soon as they were eight.

'I'm quite good in the mornings,' Cassandra responded.

'But not at night?' asked Katya, her voice suddenly soft.

'I'm usually in bed by ten,' Cassandra admitted. 'My parents always said you couldn't burn the candle at both ends.'

'How boring they sound. My parents hardly ever found time to sleep. They couldn't bear to waste a minute of their lives.'

'Do they live in England?' Cassandra asked.

Katya's eyes filled with tears – the baron could have told Cassandra that she cried crocodile tears more easily than any woman he'd ever met – and her voice dropped to a whisper. 'They died in an aeroplane crash three years ago,' she confided.

'How dreadful!' Remembering the death of her

own parents, Cassandra's easy compassion was instantly aroused.

Katya, who'd never known who her father was and whose mother had died from venereal disease shortly after she'd finished educating her twelve-year-old daughter in all the ways it was possible to please a man, let her mouth droop for a moment and then gave a brave smile. 'Well, we mustn't dwell on the past. Everyone has sadnesses in their lives. Let me take you upstairs and show you your room. It's been thoroughly spring-cleaned since Abigail left yesterday and we've changed all the curtains and bed coverings so that it fits your personality better. Dieter didn't think you and Abigail would share the same taste in interior design.'

'I really didn't expect ...' Cassandra's voice tailed off. She found it hard to imagine a man who was interested enough in his employees to change the decor of his rooms for their convenience.

'But the bedroom's so important to a woman isn't it?' Katya said, putting one small hand lightly on Cassandra's elbow as she guided her up the stairs and round to the right along the landing. 'I think it's so important to have the right kind of bedroom. Of course you've got your own little living room and bathroom, but I expect you'll be with us a lot of the time. Abigail was. She was such a success at our little dinner parties. After a few drinks she became very vivacious!'

Cassandra felt her stomach tighten a little. 'I'm afraid I'm not a dinner-party kind of person. Besides, I'm here for the children. I'm sure the baron won't want me mixing with his friends.'

'You're one of the family now,' Katya insisted. 'Don't look so nervous, dinner parties are one of the highlights of life here. Dieter knows such interesting people.'

Cassandra wished that the other woman would take her hand away from her elbow. She realised she was only trying to be friendly but the effect was rather overpowering. She felt relieved when they stopped in front of one of the heavy oak doors and Katya pushed it open. 'Here we are, your bedroom.'

Cassandra stared about her in astonishment. The bedroom was larger than the whole flat she'd just left, and it was dominated by a huge four-poster bed with apricot-coloured curtains pulled back and fastened to the posts with large oak rings. There was no quilt but instead an embroidered tapestry bedcover in gold and beige shot through with threads of the same apricot colour as the curtains. The floor was covered by a beige wool carpet so deep that you sank into it as you walked and the heavy drapes at the windows, similar in texture to those she'd seen in the drawing-room during her interview, picked up the gold thread of the bedspread. The luxurious beauty of it all distracted her from the fact that the windows were covered by heavy vertical iron bars.

Katya watched the way Cassandra's eyes lit up at the sight of the room, and she remembered that Abigail had been totally disinterested in it the day she'd arrived. Of course the colours had been different, vibrant and more obviously opulent, but her indifference should have told Katya something. As a sensualist herself she knew how important the right surroundings were, how much easier it was to be sensual in a room that pleased the eye. She had a feeling that Cassandra's slim body would also appreciate the pure silk sheets that would be changed every day, and she felt a moment's excitement as she pictured the almost boyishly slender figure sliding into bed, brushing the innocent flesh against the caresses of soft, arousing material.

'It's really lovely!' Cassandra enthused turning to Katya. She was a little surprised to find her hostess somewhat distracted and breathing unevenly, but realised that the room was hot.

'I think I'll open a window,' Cassandra said quickly.

'They don't open,' Katya interjected.

Cassandra frowned. 'Why not?'

'Well, Dieter's obsessed with the girls' safety. He's always worrying that they're going to fall off their ponies or out of windows, so most of the windows in the house are shuttered and barred. There's a fan above the bed. It works very well, we've got one in our room too, and there's also air conditioning but I'm afraid we don't use ours much. It seems to dry your throat out after a while.'

'But it's stuffy in here,' Cassandra persisted.

For a moment Katya's eyes flashed angrily, then she gave a quick smile and putting out a hand tugged gently on what Cassandra had taken to be an out-of-date bell pull. At once a huge wooden fan in the ceiling started to rotate silently, and cool air moved around them.

'See! I told you it was marvellous. When I'm hot I often lie on the bed quite naked and let it cool me down that way. You can't imagine how good it feels.'

Cassandra, who was hot and sticky by now, could imagine it very well. She found that she could also imagine Katya without her clinging micro-dress lying spreadeagled on the bed, and this made her so uncomfortable that she didn't know what to say.

Katya watched the younger woman and smiled to herself. This wasn't even going to be a contest. There were no depths to Cassandra. She was simply a surprisingly naive and as yet unawakened young woman, but there was nothing in her that would hold the baron's attention for very long. After all, it could only take a certain amount of time to spoil the innocence, and after that she couldn't imagine he'd find anything of interest in her. No, she, Katya would be the winner of this game, and she should never have lain awake half the night worrying about her opponent. From now on if she stayed awake at night it would be to plan the girl's degradation and downfall, then when the game was over she'd persuade Dieter to hand Cassandra over to Rupert for safekeeping. That way Katya would know the degradation would continue and could even, if she found a lot of pleasure in her over the next few weeks, pay the occasional visit herself. Rupert wouldn't mind.

'I'm so glad you like it,' she said brightly. 'Lucy will be up to unpack your cases in a minute. The baron will be home shortly after lunch and he'll explain what your duties are for the rest of the day. If I were you I'd have a little rest before you come down for lunch. The bathroom's through that door there; be careful, there are a couple of steps it's easy to miss.'

'Where do I go for lunch?' Cassandra asked.

'When it's nice like today we usually eat out on the back terrace. The children will join us. Their manners don't matter in the garden!'

'I thought their manners were amazing,' Cassandra protested. 'They were the politest little girls I've ever met.'

'How sweet you are.' Katya smiled again, but only with her mouth, and Cassandra took a small step away from the other woman. Suddenly she had the feeling that Katya didn't really like her, but she knew she must be mistaken because she'd been chattering away like an old friend until then and anyway Katya didn't have any reason to dislike her.

'Thank you,' Cassandra murmured.

'Oh, I didn't mean it as a compliment,' Katya replied, but before Cassandra could reply Katya had turned and left the room, letting the heavy oak door swing shut behind her.

The baron was sprawled face down on the bed, resting his chin in his hands as he kept his eyes glued to the TV set in the corner of the room. When Katya came in he didn't even acknowledge her presence, and although piqued she knew better than to try and force him to speak.

The silence in the room grew heavy with anticipation as they watched the unsuspecting Cassandra begin her exploration of the bathroom with its sunken whirlpool bath, and the baron smiled as she looked in astonishment at the wall behind the bath which was totally covered by a vast mirror. He watched as she studied herself in it, leaning forward to remove some speck of dust from her face, which was entirely free of makeup. The movement brought her so close to the concealed camera that she seemed to be looking straight into the baron's eyes and his lips parted slightly at the tranquil innocence of her gaze.

'Surely she'll take a bath,' Katya said urgently.

'Be quiet!' the baron hissed furiously. He didn't mind if Cassandra did or didn't use the bath; the very fact that only she could decide what they would see was half the excitement and Katya's voice was an unwelcome intrusion into his thoughts.

Cassandra buried her face in her hands for a moment, as though weary, and then straightened her back and stared critically at herself in the mirror. After a brief hesitation she removed the band holding her thick dark hair back off her face and shook her head. As her hair fell in a dark curtain the baron let out a tiny breath while Katya, sitting on the window seat in sullen silence, began to nibble on a carefully nurtured fingernail, a sure sign that she was agitated.

Again there was a pause, this time while Cassandra examined the taps and tried to work out how the various combination of jets worked, and then she lifted her hands and started to unbutton her safari-style cotton dress. Once the buttons were undone she shrugged it off her shoulders and let it fall to the ground behind her, then bent forward to unclasp the soft cotton bra. She then extended her arms at an angle so that this time the garment fell in front of her, leaving the secret watchers with a perfect view of her tiny breasts, their creamy pallor emphasised by the rose-coloured nipples, small tight buds more like a child's than a woman's.

The baron swallowed hard and gave a sigh of satisfaction. Katya yawned. 'She's almost flat-chested, Dieter! How boring.'

'I admit she isn't as over-ripe as your Abigail, but I'd scarcely call her flat-chested. Besides, look at that tiny waist, and her stomach. So inviting! I can just picture you with her, Katya. You'll certainly be the first woman she's ever made love with. Don't you find that exciting?'

She did, but she didn't like the look in Dieter's eyes as he stared at the screen. Abigail had never had that effect on him, and Cassandra looked so young for her twenty-three years while Katya was well aware that she looked old for her twenty-nine.

At last Cassandra stepped out of her touchingly childish white cotton panties and stepped into the bath. As she lifted her right leg, Dieter and his mistress gained their first sight of her most secret place and this time they were equally hypnotised by the screen. She had an abundance of very dark pubic hair, while the outer lips of her sex were small and tight, so that they only caught the briefest glimpse of the soft pinkness within before she sank down into the water and laid her head back against the edge of the tub.

'Do you think she'll play with herself?' Katya asked excitedly, remembering how Abigail had delighted them on her arrival.

'I would be most disappointed if she did,' the baron replied. 'This is no Abigail, my dear. Compared to your redheaded house wine this girl is a dark and mysterious claret. A rare wine and one to be savoured slowly. No, we'll get nothing more from this.' He switched off the set by remote control.

'I hadn't finished watching,' Katya exclaimed.

'Of course you had. Enjoy your lunch with her my darling, and make sure the children behave. At dinner tonight wear the sapphire blue dress with the plunging neckline, and nothing beneath it.'

'We aren't having guests are we? What does it matter what I wear?'

'The game has begun, Katya; you lose points for asking questions.'

Anger flared in Katya, but she forced it down. If Dieter thought he was annoying her he'd be delighted, and make the game more complicated. Her earlier certainty that Cassandra was no threat had vanished as they'd watched the screen. She hadn't seen such hungry desire on Dieter's face for a very long time, not since he'd first set eyes on Marietta at that wretched ball in Venice, and it had taken five long years for Marietta to vanish from the scene. Five years and her death. She had no intention of letting Cassandra stay around that long.

'You'd better get down to lunch,' the baron reminded her. Katya watched him roll onto his back, and her eyes moved down so that she could see for herself the visible sign of how Cassandra had aroused him. She moved towards the bed, watching him carefully for any sign of irritation or boredom, but there was none, simply an expression of amused tolerance.

'You really want her, don't you?' she asked quietly, sitting herself on the edge of the bed.

'Of course I do! Why else would I have employed her?'

'Tell me what you want to do to her.'

He shook his head. 'That would give too much away. Remember, this is a competition for you as well.'

'But you want to spoil her, don't you? Admit that at least. You want to change her, turn her inside out until she doesn't even recognise herself.'

The baron shrugged. 'If you say so.'

Katya ran a hand up his trouser leg and let her fingers move softly over the bulge at his crotch. 'This tells me you do.'

It was a mistake. He took her hand tightly in his and moved it away, crushing her fingers painfully together as he did so. 'Leave me alone and go down to lunch. I have to see Lucy.'

'Why?' Katya demanded.

'She and I have some unfinished business to attend to. Run along, Katya. I dislike it when you keep asking questions.' She had no choice but to leave.

Katya was in a very bad mood when Cassandra finally came into the garden to join her and the girls for lunch. She tried to disguise it, well aware that Peter, who was helping to serve the lunch, would report everything to the baron, but it was difficult to smile at the younger woman as she approached.

'I'm afraid I'm a few minutes late,' Cassandra apologised. 'I got lost and ended up in the library.'

'It doesn't matter to me, but the baron's obsessed with punctuality. You should remember that in future,' Katya said, signalling for the maid to pass round the plates.

'Of course. I expect I'll soon find my way around. The trouble was, there wasn't anyone to ask. Where do the staff hide away? I never see anyone!'

'They keep to their quarters. Helena, sit up straight and put your plate on your knees. Didn't Abigail teach you anything?'

The four-year-old glanced at Katya from beneath lowered lids. 'Not much,' she said quietly. 'She was always disappearing into your room.'

Katya turned to Cassandra. 'I'm afraid Abigail was rather taken with my clothes and makeup. I often caught her in the bedroom on some flimsy pretext or other. I suppose you have to feel sorry for someone like that but it wasn't nice. That's why she had to go.'

Cassandra's eyes widened. 'Really? The baron said something about her not being keen enough on discipline.'

'Well, there was that too, but really she was thoroughly untrustworthy. The agency chose her for us. This time the baron insisted on doing the interviewing himself. So much wiser I think.'

Cassandra nodded. 'You do need to meet people before you can . . .' She stopped as a strange cry pierced the air. It wasn't like the one she'd heard on her previous visit; there was no suggestion of pain in the sound, but it disturbed Cassandra. She glanced at Katya to see if she'd heard it. The other woman's face had gone very white and for a second she was quite motionless, but then her hands busied themselves with her food and her colour returned.

'Yes, I agree,' she continued smoothly. 'It's always better to meet people face to face. You can learn so much from expressions, don't you think?' Her green eyes stared straight into Cassandra's. The effect was hypnotic. The younger woman felt unable to look away, and as she stared at Katya she began to feel strange. Her limbs started to feel heavy, and as her shoulders relaxed she felt a peculiar sensation in the pit of her stomach. Katya leant towards her, putting out a tiny, multi-ringed hand and moving it towards Cassandra's knee. 'You know, Cassandra, there are things I . . .'

Helena, staring at her father's mistress in fascination, let her legs slip to one side and the plate fell from her knees and shattered on the patio. The crash of breaking china jolted Cassandra back into the present, and Katya leapt to her feet in a fury.

'You stupid, stupid child! Look what you've done. You wait until I tell your papa about this. He'll be very angry and you'll be punished, won't she Cassandra? I'm quite sure Cassandra knows the right punishment for careless, clumsy, ugly little girls like you.'

Helena's big blue eyes filled with tears and she clasped her hands together in her lap. 'I didn't mean to,' she whispered. 'It was an accident.'

Christina, apparently unperturbed by her older sister's tears, looked up at the word accident. 'Mama's dead,' she said clearly. 'It was an accident.'

'Be quiet, Christina!' Katya's voice was lower now, but unmistakably menacing and Christina shrank away from her.

'I didn't mean to,' Helena repeated, her bottom lip trembling as she looked at Cassandra.

'Don't worry,' Cassandra said quickly. 'We all have accidents from time to time.'

'Goodness me, I'm afraid you won't last long,' Katya said, her anger suddenly draining away. 'Dieter wouldn't approve of that sentiment at all.'

'But she's only four!' Cassandra said, longing to put her arms round the little girl but not sure if she should. 'It isn't as though she threw it deliberately.'

'I want her punished,' Katya said flatly. 'That's all there is to it. She spoilt the lunch.'

'Good afternoon ladies! Is there some kind of problem?' asked a masculine voice, and the baron walked lightly up the steps from the French windows to the patio.

'That clumsy daughter of yours has just broken a piece of the dinner service,' Katya said spitefully. 'She didn't like it because I was talking to Cassandra and she wanted some attention.'

Shocked, Cassandra opened her mouth to protest but then closed it again. She'd only just arrived. She couldn't possibly contradict the baron's fiancée in front of him, and yet it was all so ridiculous and unfair and she knew it was her job to put across the child's point of view. She tried to think how she could tell the baron the truth without appearing to contradict Katya.

'Helena, is this true?' the baron asked his daughter.

Helena hung her head and fiddled with her fingers.

'Answer me, is it true?'

'It was an accident,' his daughter whispered.

Christina tugged at her father's jacket. 'Mama's dead,' she reminded him. His eyes moved quickly from the tiny two-year-old to the watching Cassandra, and suddenly he smiled. 'It's too nice a day to spoil with an argument. I think we'll forget it this time. Peter, clear the mess up. Katya, your masseur's arrived. Lucy will take the children upstairs for a nap while I have a talk with Cassandra here.'

As the girls scampered away and Peter began to sweep up the broken china, Cassandra glanced at Katya and saw that she was absolutely furious. Her eyes were glinting with anger and her mouth was a thin, tight line while two vivid spots of colour stood out on her cheeks.

'Katya, your masseur,' the baron reminded her.

'I wanted her punished,' Katya said icily. 'She spoilt . . .'

'I know exactly what she spoilt,' he said. His voice was low and didn't carry to Cassandra. 'You had no business to try and seduce her over lunch. I am not pleased with you.' He raised his voice again. 'Hurry up, darling. You know how Pierre hates to be kept waiting.'

'That's just too bad,' Katya snapped, and she walked slowly back towards the house, emphasising the fact that she intended to keep him waiting.

Cassandra stood up and waited for the baron to speak. She'd thought about him a lot since the interview, and now that she was facing him again her heart was beating rather too fast and she felt ridiculously pleased to see him. He smiled at her, almost as though he was equally pleased to see her.

'Katya always makes a terrible drama out of everything. Now you can see why she would not make a good mother substitute.'

'I expect it's difficult to take on two little girls,' Cassandra said.

'Ah, you play the diplomat! Very good, my dear. But tell me, what was the truth of it all? Did Helena want attention or was it an accident?'

Cassandra took some steadying breaths and looked straight at her employer, determined to be truthful with him from the start. 'I thought it was an accident. It isn't easy to balance plates on knees even when you're an adult.'

'Good!'

'Also, she was very upset. Usually when children want attention they make scenes, but they don't shed real tears, just tears of fury.'

'So Katya lied?' he asked softly.

'No, I'm sure she thought it was deliberate.'

'Are you?'

Cassandra was confused. Actually she wasn't sure. It had seemed to her that Katya had been furious about something else and had taken it out on the little girl, at the same time taking a perverse pleasure in the child's distress, but she knew she couldn't possibly say that. 'Perhaps there are undercurrents between the two of them that I don't know about,' she said at last.

The baron nodded his approval. 'Well said. Perhaps there are many complexities of emotion in this house that you have yet to learn about, but that will all be part of your education won't it? You plainly have an abundance of commonsense as well as all the other more obvious virtues.'

His eyes travelled down her body and then back up again, quite slowly and without any attempt to disguise his appraisal. Cassandra was amazed to find that she didn't mind, that she even stood slightly straighter beneath his gaze. When he looked into her eyes again his expression was neutral. 'I think you will do very well,' he commented, almost to himself, then he put out a hand, touched her lightly on the cheek and turned back to the house. 'There is a timetable in your room. Study it and then commence your duties. You will dine with us at nine tonight. The children should be asleep by then, and if they do wake one of the nursery staff will see to them. Dress is formal.'

Left alone in the garden, Cassandra felt totally confused. She'd expected a long talk with the baron while he outlined the way in which he wanted her to structure his daughters' days; instead, he'd spent no more than five minutes with her in which nothing had really been said and yet she felt strangely changed.

Now that he'd gone she could still feel the gentle touch of his fingers on her cheek, and recall the way his eyes had scrutinised her, and how her body had tightened beneath his gaze in a way it had never tightened when Paul, her ex-boyfriend, had looked at her.

Even now her nipples felt hard against the fabric of her bra, and she was more aware of her body than she'd ever been. The long skirt that she was wearing seemed to be brushing insistently against her legs and without realising what she was doing she moved her hands down over her hips and thighs, just as Katya had done when she came down the stairs towards her that morning. It felt good, and she lifted her face to the sky and let the sun's rays touch her face, warming it until the glow began to spread down her throat as well.

From an upstairs window, Dieter von Ritter watched the tall, slim young woman as for the first time she began to be aware of her body as something that needed more than food and clothing and his own body stirred. When he'd let his eyes travel over her he'd been picturing her as she'd been on the screen, her unawakened body pale and slim and, best of all, unaware of what was to come.

That had been all he'd expected to get from the examination, a quick frisson of pleasure, but it had become much more. She'd seemed to come alive beneath his very gaze. He'd seen how the pulse beneath her ear had started to quicken and he'd known then that this was going to be a very special game. It was going to take every ounce of his self-discipline not to hurry her through the tests, but he knew that the savouring of each moment should be extended to give them all the maximum amount of pleasure possible. And pain too of course, but to him they were the same thing, and they would be to Cassandra, he was sure of that now. There would be no repetition of the tears and pathetic whimperings of Abigail. No, this girl would understand and rise to the challenge. It was a long time since he had felt such excitement.

The Captive Flesh

Cleo Cordell

Cleo Cordell's name has become almost synonymous with the Black Lace brand. She has written seven books for the imprint; each one having a dark, gothic flavour. She specialises in historical fiction and cites Anne Rice and Tanith Lee as two of her influences.

The Captive Flesh was one of the first Black Lace books and is set in the sun-drenched opulence of an Algerian mansion. French convent girls Marietta and Claudine are rescued by the handsome Kasim and invited to stay at his home. But they soon realise that he requires something from them in return for his hospitality: their complete surrender to pleasure and pain.

Juliet Rising is set in a strict 18th-century ladies' academy where young girls are taught in the ways of deportment, manners and how to bend handsome young men to their will. Madame Nicol runs a tight ship and will brook no nonsense, but she has their best interests at heart. The wilful Juliet is an eager pupil and cannot wait to practise her newly-learnt skills of discipline on the besotted young Reynard.

Other Black Lace books by Cleo Cordell are: *The Senses Bejewelled* (the sequel to *The Captive Flesh*), *Velvet Claws* (set in Africa before the turn of the century), *Path of the Tiger* (set in India, in the days of the Raj), *The Crimson Buccaneer* (set in Imperial Spain) and *Opal Darkness* (set in Europe in the 1860s).

The Captive Flesh

Marietta bowed her head and slipped on the short transparent waistcoat. The sides barely covered her nipples and were linked with a gold chain. The garment was designed to draw attention to her breasts rather than conceal them. From the waist down, she was to remain naked. The little gold device that cinched her sex was clearly visible.

Everyone else in the harem was dressed in loose trousers and tunics or gowns. She felt horribly self-conscious and set apart from them all. Which, of course, was Kasim's intention. Leyla gave her no immediate orders so she decided to make her way to her sleeping cubicle. There she could close the curtains around her bed and hide herself away for a while.

In the corridor, she passed a slave girl holding a pile of linen. Lowering her eyes she made to walk past, but the slave girl dropped her burden and rounded on Marietta.

'You. French woman. Stand still,' she said in peremptory tone.

Too surprised to refuse, Marietta paused. Whereupon the slave moved close to her, grinning in a way that lacked any respect.

'Stand for me!' she said again, and reaching out, stroked Marietta's bare buttocks.

Another slave, passing by carrying a jug of sherbet, reached out and took hold of Marietta's gold waist chain. She snapped the chain between her fingers, pulling it up high so that the mesh was pulled even tighter between Marietta's legs. Marietta gave a sound of protest. Both slaves laughed. The first stuck her tongue out, picked up her pile of linen, and walked away with insolent slowness. Marietta pulled free and ran away, her heart beating fast.

Just before she reached the bed chamber two more slaves stopped her. Again she was ordered to stand still. One of the slaves pushed her against a wall and held her wrists above her head. The other opened her waistcoat and began roughly to fondle her breasts. When Marietta cried out in alarm a hand was clamped tightly to her mouth. A voice close to her ear mouthed an obscenity, laughing huskily.

Her nipples were pinched until they were sore and then her breasts were slapped until she sobbed with the warm ache in them.

'Stop. Please. Stop ... Why are you doing this?' she moaned against the fingers that forced her mouth open and tugged at her underlip.

Ignoring her, one of them stroked the mesh that covered her sex. Marietta was ashamed at the rush of sensation that rose in her. The grip on her wrists, her hands pressed flat to the cold wall, reminded her of how Kasim had secured her to the marble pillar. The hand at her sex pressed harder, slapping with a gentle but eager pleasure. A slim finger traced the outline of the cage, lifting the edge so that it could tease out the golden curls within.

Marietta writhed. Her breasts burned and her sex throbbed maddeningly. She could not help thrusting her hips towards the teasing fingers. They were withdrawn abruptly.

'Naughty. Naughty,' the slave smirked, and slapped her buttocks hard. Marietta almost wept with humiliation. She hated the way she responded to their rough treatment. She bit her lip and began to struggle against the grip on her wrists. But the slaves only laughed harder as she tried to jerk free.

'Not so high and mighty now are you French woman?' they teased, making free with her in whatever way they wished.

Marietta closed her eyes, enduring the pinches and slaps, holding back the tears of pain. Until, tiring of tormenting her at last, the two slaves sauntered away. When they had gone Marietta sagged against the wall, shaking and afraid.

'This is how it will be until you are willing to do as you are told,' Leyla told her later. 'While you wear the caging device anyone may handle you as they wish. Your status now is that of a slave. You must obey all commands. To refuse will earn you a spanking or worse.'

Marietta hung her head, blushing furiously. How would she bear it? There was a wicked delight to be had in being the object of so much attention, as she had found already. But the cage ensured that she was denied any pleasure. It was cruel. Oh, Kasim, she thought, you know how beguiling all this is. You are testing me still, willing me to become your creature. But you will not break me.

'It is hard for me to resist you,' Leyla whispered. 'Your flushed face moves me greatly. I am tempted to free your pretty sex ... I dare not. Yet I must touch you ...'

Leyla clasped Marietta in her arms and kissed her. Marietta responded ardently as Leyla ran her hands gently over her sore breasts and buttocks. With a shuddering breath Leyla put Marietta from her.

'You will make me forget my duty. Come, I must teach you the many ways to please a man. Kasim will test you and punish you further if you do not find favour with him.'

Over the next few days Leyla showed Marietta the ways to draw out pleasure from a man's body with dance, hands, lips, and tongue. Despite her initial resistance she enjoyed her lessons. For everything she learned seemed designed to tantalise and delight her own senses also.

It was also impossible to remain unmoved by all the luxury around her. The colours of tiles, stained-glass, and rich furnishings delighted her eyes. The harem was filled with the smells of incense, exotic musky perfumes, and fruit blossom. She was served soft eggs with cream and sliced fresh figs for breakfast. Later there were fragrant lamb stews, fish stuffed with almonds, soups flavoured with cumin, artichokes in oil. All this was followed by squares of sweet rice jelly sprinkled with rosewater,

water lily sherbet with violets and honey, and the many sticky sweetmeats with voluptuous names. There was the thick sweet coffee and Russian tea to drink.

After the plain fare of the convent, Marietta ate and drank with relish. Soft music soothed her to sleep. The cries of peacocks floated into the open windows on hot damp nights. There seemed no escape from luxury, no way to avoid the pleasures of all the senses.

Marietta was kept busy with her lessons and with avoiding the slaves who took every opportunity to fondle her. She did not see Claudine for some days. At first, she was not unduly worried. The harem was a warren of corridors, ornate rooms, and secret gardens. It was not difficult to lose oneself. She assumed that Claudine was being trained also. But when Claudine's bed space remained empty one morning, Marietta began to get worried.

Then she heard the women whispering and glancing sidelong at her. One of the slaves, a thin severe-looking girl, who singled her out regularly for special intimate attentions, told her that Claudine was keeping Kasim's bed warm. The slave relished passing on the information, while she smacked Marietta's breasts and buttocks, only smiling when Marietta paled and called her a liar.

'But surely you are not jealous? Perhaps you think your friend finds more favour with Kasim than you?'

Marietta dismissed the slave's words. Of course she was not jealous. She was just worried about Claudine. What would happen when Kasim tired of her? Would he then turn his attentions back to herself?

Kasim came often to the harem unannounced. Late one evening he appeared, looking striking in a loose white linen shirt and full trousers tucked into high boots. Leyla and Marietta were alone. The lessons for the day had just been completed. Leyla greeted him deferentially. Kasim beckoned Marietta to stand close. He checked first that the cage was secure. After toying with her waist chain, his long fingers trailing down the curve of her hip, he ignored her and spoke to Leyla.

'She has not been pleasured by anyone or herself? You are certain of this? Was she watched during sleep?'

'Yes, my lord. Though she burns she has not been sated.'

'Good. Very good. The banquet is tomorrow night. I want her hot and ready. She has completed her training as I ordered?'

'Yes, my lord,' Leyla answered. 'As you have seen these past weeks, she has been diligent.'

'Diligent? Hmmm. But is she obedient enough I wonder? I would test her. On your knees, Marietta,' he ordered suddenly. 'Show me how you would pleasure a man with your mouth.'

Kasim made himself comfortable on a divan and sipped at a glass of cherry sherbet.

Marietta arranged herself into the required position; shoulders back, hands linked behind her, and her knees spread widely apart. Leyla stood to one side, holding a carved ivory phallus. Kasim watched closely as Marietta opened her mouth and took the head of the phallus between her lips.

Trying not to think of his dark eyes on her, Marietta worked her mouth up and down the phallus. She closed her eyes briefly, concentrating on performing as she had been taught. I must make my lips loose, peel them back over the rim of the plum, then suck gently as I slide my mouth down the shaft.

'Sit up straight,' Kasim ordered. 'Thrust out those breasts.'

The gold chain tightened around her waist and bit into her flesh-valley as Marietta obeyed. Her buttocks too were thrust out by her position. She felt intensely vulnerable, knowing that Kasim was gazing on all the secret parts of her body. The fine open-work mesh fitted closely to her mound, out-lining rather than concealing the shape of her sex.

Kasim admired the look of it. 'Your pretty curls protrude through the mesh and I can see the shadow of your parted flesh-lips. It really is tanta-lising. Perhaps I shall imprison your breasts in this way too. Ah, how lovely they would look with their fullness contained and yet revealed, with your nipples pushing against the gold mesh. The metal would chafe and excite them . . .'

Marietta lowered her chin, concentrating on suck-ing the phallus. She closed her eyes against the sudden intensity of his face. An image of Kasim pleasuring Claudine flashed into her head. Clau-dine knew how his full mouth tasted, his skin, his cock . . . Claudine had seen those hard dark eyes brighten with desire for her. Marietta felt consumed by a mixture of emotions.

Kasim watched her silently as she drew the thick pale shaft in and out of her mouth. His face was unreadable. She gave a little shiver. Perhaps he would wish her to practice on his erect phallus. Her cheeks warmed with anticipation. How would he taste? She longed for the scent of his skin in her nostrils. For the feel of him under her hands, her lips.

She was damp already between her thighs. For days she had been aroused, shadowed by the presence of the horrid little cage clasped so firmly around her sex. The pressure of it was both a deterrent and a potent reminder of her leashed sexuality.

The ivory phallus had warmed in her mouth. It felt smooth and so hard. She circled it with her tongue and flashed Kasim a look from the tail of her eye. The gold chain, pulled tight between her buttocks, began rubbing at her flesh-valley as she moved slightly. Never had her body seemed so beyond her control. Never had she hungered so for anyone's touch.

Kasim laughed suddenly. 'She is ready. Almost. You have done well, Leyla. Make her beautiful. I will return for the final preparation.'

Marietta spent hours in the hammam being steamed, scrubbed with pumice and massaged. Every part of her, except her sex, was stroked and kneaded. Exotic perfumes were rubbed into her skin with long and languorous strokes.

The intimate attentions were a form of torture to her. The weeks of training, the teasing and spankings had stirred her to a fever pitch of arousal. Leyla watched her carefully, gauging her reactions. Marietta felt an echo of her own leashed torment in the Turkish woman's demeanour. Only Kasim's

160

express orders had stopped them exploring each other's bodies in the dark scented night.

Marietta held her breath when the little mesh cage was removed so that her sex might be cleansed.

'Draw up your legs and hold your knees apart,' Leyla said.

Marietta did so, feeling Leyla's long dark eyes on her. Warm scented water was poured over her open flesh-lips. Marietta almost moaned aloud, filled with unbearable tension. Her hips began to work as she strained towards the warm, caressing flow. Leyla ordered the slave to stop pouring.

'Direct the water away from the pulsing bud of pleasure,' Leyla said.

The stream was redirected when Marietta had gained control. She almost wept with frustration. Leyla only smiled and kissed her lightly on the mouth. 'I understand. I feel it too. But the waiting is almost over. Now we must decorate your body.'

Marietta felt a sweet heavy ache as her pubic curls were brushed, teased, and oiled, until they stood out in a glistening curly halo.

'I regret having to do this,' Leyla said softly as she replaced the gold mesh between Marietta's thighs and secured it to the waist chain. She fluffed out the golden curls so that they protruded around the sides and top of the mesh.

'Only Kasim can order the cage's removal. Take care that you please him when he next orders it. And he will free you.'

Marietta felt a fierce joy at the thought. When would he order her to pleasure him? What would he make her do? Her thoughts seemed crowded with him. After so much time, when she had seen him only as a fleeting visitor, she longed to be alone with him. For him to take her to his apartments. Perhaps to secure her wrists to that slim marble pillar . . .

She sat still while her nipples were rouged; her hands and feet decorated with henna. Then her hair was brushed out so that it hung free in a cascade of silver curls. The tresses were perfumed with musk-rose oil, then threaded with gold chains and looped with ropes of pearls.

When Marietta was ready, Kasim came into the harem. At a sign from him Marietta assumed the posture of submission. Without a word he reached for the chain at her waist and removed the cage.

Then he ordered her to lie on her back on a nearby divan. There was a small knot of excitement in her stomach. She did as he asked, lying back and parting her legs. He made a small sound of appreciation. Still without speaking, he took a small jar and dipped his fingers into it. Then he reached between her legs and began to anoint her flesh-lips with a spicy scented oil. Already aroused, she trembled like a leaf in the wind.

Kasim's dark eyes gleamed. A satisfied smile played over his hard mouth. The touch of his fingers maddened her. The pressure was firm, almost impersonal, but so welcome that she felt her sex-lips become liquid. Her sex felt heavily engorged. She knew that her outside flesh-lips were full and pouting, resembling a firm plum. She closed her eyes, feeling her pleasure mounting. A moment more and she would climax. The tips of Kasim's fingers probed inside her, then brushed lightly over her pleasure bud, anointing it with the spicy oil.

It was too much. She broke all at once. The waves rolled over her in great wrenching spasms, consuming her, blinding her to everything but the moment.

'Oh, oh,' she gasped as her womb convulsed. Her thighs closed on Kasim's hand as she rubbed shamelessly on his fingers. His hand closed over her sex, pinching the lips together hard as if he could stop the pleasure which was only now beginning to ebb. She pressed towards him with a little sob, hearing him curse under his breath, but not caring that she had lost control. It was some moments before she recovered. The afterglow was sweet but brief. Her thighs fell open as lassitude spread over her limbs.

Kasim frowned and withdrew his hand. His mouth was a hard line. Then he smiled and, leaning over, brushed her lips with his. 'You should be spanked for that loss of control, but I feel generous this night. Besides, I should not have handled you so gently. I will allow you that one moment of delight. Wait ... Give me your mouth.'

Marietta lifted her chin and pursed her lips. Kasim swept his finger over her mouth. She tasted sweet spices and her own musk, before her lips grew warm and swollen.

'Now, get up,' Kasim said.

Only then did she become aware that the whole of her sex and flesh-valley felt warm and tingling, the same as her mouth. Her erect bud throbbed with almost painful intensity. It did not seem possible, but Kasim's touch had brought her to an even more extreme state of heightened arousal. Her release of a moment before had done nothing to assuage her desire.

'There,' Kasim replaced the lid on the little jar. 'That mixture of spices I rubbed into your sex and mouth will ensure that you remain so hungry for pleasure that you care not who gives it. But your task this night is to *give* pleasure only. All you have to do is obey me. You will hunger, but you will not be eased. See that you hold yourself back. For I warn you. I shall not forgive another lapse. Your pleasure must wait until I order you to take it. Do you understand?'

She managed to nod, her thoughts in a turmoil.

'Good. The guests are about to arrive. Follow me.'

Kasim's private apartments had been transformed for the banquet.

Candles in stained-glass containers cast pools of green, blue, and red light on to the rich carpet, while the corners of the large room were in complete darkness. The divans around the central cleared area were filled with guests. Others stood around the room chatting, helping themselves to food from small tables. All the guests were richly dressed in silks and brocades. Jewels flashed from turbans and sashes. Slaves moved to and fro serving glasses of sherbet from gold and silver trays.

Marietta was displayed prominently, chained to the marble pillar as before, this time in the submissive posture. Guests walked around her, lifting up her long hair, feeling the weight of her breasts, murmuring idle compliments. Now and then she felt the stroke of a thin cane between her legs. Her nipples were stroked until they became erect. The many touches, the small attentions, were light, careless, almost throwaway, as if she was of little account. She suffered them in silence, betraying her reactions by shuddering very slightly. The sense of being worthless was deeply humiliating but exciting too. How did Kasim always know how to reach inside the deepest recesses of her mind and draw her out, expose her darkest desires, and make her ever more naked to him?

She began to long for the casual attentions of the guests, but wished that she could dip her chin, so that she need not see their faces. They all looked so smug, so soft with good living. Perhaps she could hide her face with the heavy fall of her hair, but a stiff gold collar set with pearls and moonstones prevented it. The number of people, the noise, terrified her. She had somehow imagined that Kasim would take her to his apartments and use her for his pleasure alone. But she and Claudine were to remain on show, displayed like the prized ornaments they were.

Claudine was chained in similar fashion to the marble pillar opposite. Her friend looked magnificent. She did not look afraid and seemed to be enjoying all the attention. Like Marietta she was naked and arranged in the posture of submission. Above a high collar of gold, set with cornelians and rubies, her chin was thrust out haughtily. The wide golden-brown eyes flicked over the guests with interest. The thick red-gold hair, threaded with strings of rubies, tumbled over her naked shoulders.

Claudine smiled at Marietta. Her eyes looked

dreamy and unfocused. She stretched luxuriously and arched her back. Marietta saw the newly naked sex, the outer lips agape, and the inner flesh-lips hanging down slightly. She saw how red and wet the sex was and realised that Claudine too had been anointed with spicy oil. As Claudine thrust her full breasts forward, Marietta noticed for the first time that Claudine's pale-brown nipples were encircled by gold rings. Somehow the erect nipples had been teased through the tiny rings so that they remained hard and engorged. The tender nipple-skin was shiny, elongated into a tiny jutting teat, collared by the unresisting metal.

Though she resisted the thought, Marietta found herself imagining wearing such rings. Could she bear that pressure, the exquisite feeling of constriction? Claudine seemed proud to wear them. Had Kasim forced them on her? His cruelty was unrelenting. Marietta shivered as she remembered his hard fingers working the spicy oil into her secret flesh.

Just then a rather handsome merchant with gold teeth smiled at Marietta, distracting her from studying her friend. Moving aside his full-skirted robe, he stroked the bulge at his groin, at the same time cupping her chin and squeezing her cheeks so that her mouth opened. Marietta blushed violently. The merchant crowed with delight and freed his erect penis, pressing forward so that the tip pressed against her lips.

His cock was long and rather thin. The tip was naked with a pronounced collar of flesh around the plum. As her mouth closed over the warm swollen tip and she began sucking, she lowered her eyelids, glad to shut out the sight of his shiny red face and lustful eyes. But it seemed that even that luxury was not allowed her. Kasim appeared at her side.

'Your pardon, my friend,' he said to the merchant, who drew away regretfully, his own hand continuing to pump his cock-stem.

'Ah, you must chastise this disobedient slave?' The merchant grinned. 'No matter. I will use the other's mouth.'

Claudine accommodated the merchant's hardness with relish. While he plundered Claudine's throat, the merchant turned his head so that he might watch Kasim's actions.

'This night you are to look the guests in the eye as you pleasure them,' Kasim said to Marietta.

Marietta was confused. Normally, in the posture of submission, she was made to keep her eyes lowered. She tried to stammer a reply, but her hesitancy was taken for resistance.

'Do you not answer your master? Then take this for your disobedience,' Kasim rapped, beginning to slap the under-swell of her breasts.

He slapped each breast in turn, snapping their weight upwards until they glowed with warmth. Marietta twisted and sobbed as his hand connected again and again. Each time he allowed the breast to drop before he slapped it again, so that the bruising ache added to her torment. She had never been slapped in that way before. It seemed that she was consumed by a mixture of pleasure-pain. Her whole body shook. She squeezed her thighs together and felt her sex pulse as the oiled flesh-lips closed together. Her nipples contracted to hard little nubs like pink stone. She began to moan between the sobs, the sound supplicating even to her own ears. Something within her reached out to Kasim. In his beautiful hard face, the set of his mouth, she sensed that he was highly aroused and she felt glad that she could stir him to such a pitch.

The merchant nearby groaned with pleasure as Marietta's flushed face became streaked with tears. He plunged himself into Claudine's mouth until he climaxed with a hoarse groan. A small group had gathered to watch Kasim chastise Marietta. She heard the sighs of pleasure, the comments on her beauty. The watchers drew away a little as Kasim stood back and lowered his hand.

Marietta sagged. She bent over at the waist as if she could shield her tormented breasts from the sea of eyes. She sobbed without restraint as the warm pain flooded her breasts. Her belly jerked with the force of her distress ... but inside her there was a hard peak of excitement. She was frightened by the delicious drowning feeling of submission. It had come stronger this time. Stronger even than when Kasim had lashed her in front of Leyla.

Kasim ran his hands over the vibrantly blushing breasts, squeezing hard and holding them up. He admired their colour. The pink nipples, cresting the dark-rose flesh, were startling in contrast. There were murmurs of approval and admiration from the watching guests. Kasim tugged on the chain attached to Marietta's beautiful gold collar, so that she straightened up further and was forced to lift her chin even higher.

'Keep your head high, Marietta,' he hissed. 'Thrust out those breasts so that everyone can admire them, and keep those legs well spread. I want all my guests to enjoy your beauty.'

Marietta bit her trembling lips. A final sob was forced from her as she opened her knees wide, pushing backwards until the joints at her groin ached.

'Good. Good,' Kasim said gently. 'Now you are obedient.'

He tweaked her pubic curls, rubbing the oiled strands between his fingers, fluffing them up and stroking them back from the exposed and parted sex. Marietta felt herself bear down. Her sex seemed to push out. She managed to stop herself swaying towards his hand only with a great effort. Her sex burned, and throbbed, yearning for any contact. It seemed that all her thoughts of rebellion, her wish for freedom, had sunk somewhere below her immediate consciousness. There was only the heat in her breasts, the hungry ache in her belly, the craving for sexual release.

Kasim patted her head then left her and walked over to Claudine. Claudine smiled, anticipating his approval. She licked her lips as if still tasting the merchant's thin milt. She brought her hands forward and placed them on her thighs. The fingers, spread and pointing inwards, drew attention to her hot little sex. As Kasim stopped in front of her, Claudine drew in her belly and looked up at him through lowered lashes. She thrust her hips forward, so that the little purse of her naked sex was lifted invitingly.

Kasim's mouth thinned. 'You are too eager! Hands behind your back,' he said, and pinched her nipples until she gasped with pain.

Hurriedly she clasped her hands behind her back. Kasim slapped her large breasts hard. Once, twice, three times on the out-swell of each breast. Claudine's mouth opened with shock. It was plain that she had not been chastised in this way before. Marietta felt sorry for Claudine but her whole body had pulsed with pleasure as she watched Kasim slap the rich outer curves. The upper-swell and deep cleavage of Claudine's breasts remained their normal shade of light-gold, speckled with freckles; while the outer slopes – pulled taut by the held back shoulders – were flushed deep-rose. The effect was most enticing. Claudine's lovely mouth trembled violently and her eyes watered.

'You should know better by now. What are you? Tell me,' Kasim's voice was deceptively gentle as he waited for the reply that did not come fast enough. He reached between Claudine's thighs and tapped the parted flesh-lips with two fingers, spanking the tender exposed flesh smartly.

'Your . . . your obedient servant,' Claudine whispered, finding her voice. She winced and writhed as he grasped the whole of her sex and pinched the naked lips together. Tremors passed across her belly.

'See that you remember that at all times,' Kasim rapped, removing his hand. He strode across the room and began speaking to one of his guests.

Claudine stared after Kasim, her face flushed and tear-stained. She still looked shocked. Glancing at Marietta, she whispered in a shaky voice:

'I thought I was special . . . that after the past few days. . . But he treats me like a common slave . . .'

Marietta understood. It seemed that sharing

Kasim's bed did not raise one's status. She was inexplicably glad of the fact, but she trembled with fear. Kasim appeared so cold, so detached. What else would he expect of them? Was it not enough that they must display their naked bodies to all those lewd gazes; make their mouths available to whoever wished to use them; and be forced to look into the eyes of each lustful guest? Even now she felt the merchants' eyes on her rounded arms and shoulders, on her breasts, and especially between her thighs.

She had heard the many comments and the laughter. Some of the merchants were fascinated by her difference, others were appalled.

'Have you seen the pale slave? The new girl?'

'Beautiful, is she not? Such pretty breasts.'

'Yes. But she has hair on her sex! Disgraceful!'

'I agree. But it's rather compelling. So pale and fine. One feels driven to feel it. To taste it. What must it feel like to plunge into a sex with hair on?'

'Ah, yes. Or to bury one's fingers inside that pretty fleshpot while plundering her tight little anus.'

'You only have to ask Kasim. He'll let you sample the goods. Is he not famous for his generosity?'

Marietta blanched at the last comment. Surely Kasim would not give her over to be used in that way. The thought of being penetrated, of her shrinking flesh sleeving those hard male organs while others watched, horrified and tantalised her. She knew that she would not be able to help showing her pleasure if anyone used her so intimately. How terrible to have to hold herself back as Kasim had ordered. But how much more awful to be viewed with her back arched, her buttocks working shamelessly, and her avid bud grinding against whatever flesh-surface presented itself.

Although much time had passed since Kasim anointed her with spicy oil, she was still at a peak of intense arousal. The breast spanking had only added to the feeling. How wet and swollen her sex was. The normally pink flesh must be shockingly red and plump. It seemed dreadful that her open flesh-lips, the mouth of her central orifice, and the tormented swollen bud, were spread so wide to the hungry gaze of Kasim's guests.

Once she had hated the gold cage that masked her sex, now she wished for it back. If only she could crawl into a dark corner and hide. Her rosy breasts throbbed and tingled, but she must still bear the strokes and pinches of the guests. Now and then she must suck an erect cock, or suffer a mouth to cover hers and a thrusting tongue to circle the inside of her lips, questing for the last faint taste of some other's salty emission. And all of this was viewed by so many. Her expertise, her willingness, her physical perfection, everything was commented on. Oh, there could be nothing in the world worse than this.

And yet it was all so arousing.

Juliet Rising

Cleo Cordell

Juliet Rising

Juliet stood in the centre of the old dance studio.
The room looked as it always did except for the
addition of a black, wrought iron table. On the table
was a white vase, filled with lilies.

The scent of the flowers, sweet and dusty, filled
the room. Juliet turned slowly towards the door as
she heard sounds echo through the wide corridor.
Yes, there were footsteps drawing nearer. Facing
the door, she waited.

'Ah, Reynard. You're here. Come in,' she said
and gave him a smile of welcome.

She saw his eyes widen as he took in the details
of her dress. The slow colour filled his cheeks. How
satisfying it was to see his mouth grow slack and
his eyes darken with desire. He had not noticed
what she held in her hand. All his attention was
centred on her body; on the black velvet corset,
laced so tightly and curved at the top to leave her
breasts completely bare.

A full white skirt was looped over wide panniers and caught up at the front to show her slender legs and rounded thighs. Black leather boots were laced to her knees. She inclined her head, loving the weight of the black top hat with its veil of spotted net. Apart from the refinements, her outfit was a classic riding costume.

'You look ... wonderful,' Reynard said, the words seeming to catch in his throat.

'I'm glad you approve,' she said dryly. 'Come here if you please. The lesson is about to begin.'

Only then did Reynard notice what she held in her hand. The truth of his situation seemed to dawn on him for the first time. He hid his panic well. She saw him glance nervously towards the open door and raised her eyebrow.

'Thinking of leaving?'

He shook his head. When he spoke again his voice was rough with suppressed passion.

'No,' he said, lifting his head and walking towards the table.

'Good. Then disrobe, at once. Ah, here are Madame and Estelle. They are here to help with the lesson. But it is I who will take charge today. Now Reynard. We begin.'

Reynard slowly unbuttoned his brown cord frock coat. His fingers were stiff and a little clumsy. Part of him wanted to leave at once and hurry back to Justin's house, but a larger part of him was bound by a dark fascination.

He knew that he had been tricked. This was not what he'd come for. He'd had some vague notion of sitting in on one of Madame's lessons, perhaps speaking to the pupils and impressing them with his charm. He'd fancied that there'd be an opportunity to get to know Juliet better too.

This was quite a different matter, but he'd given his word and it was not in his nature to backtrack on a promise. Besides, if he was honest, now that he'd glimpsed what Madame's private lessons would actually entail he found himself unable to react in any forceful way. Whether there was an element of pride or honour in his demeanour he didn't know, but something far more basic kept him rooted to the floor while he undressed in front of the watching women.

The simple fact was that he had never been so aroused, nor so intrigued, in the whole of his life.

Madame and Estelle stood by, neither of them speaking. Was this a commonplace event for them? Reynard was acutely aware of their presence, but his eyes hardly left Juliet. He wasn't prepared for her, or for the way she looked today.

Somehow he had assumed she would be wearing the plain, unflattering school uniform, not this startling, altogether shocking outfit.

She stood straight-backed, looking slightly down her nose at him as he removed his coat and began loosening the linen stock at his throat. He was fascinated by the set of her head and the graceful sweep of her bare neck and shoulders. Her dark hair had been coiled and secured in a net low at her nape. The spotted veil on the top hat masked her face, giving her expression a certain mystery.

He tried to see her eyes, to see what her reaction to his presence was, but it was impossible. Only her mouth and rounded chin were uncovered. Ah, that mouth. Surely it was too soft, too voluptuous for a person with such a strong character. How deceptive that mouth was.

He pulled off his knee-length leather boots and began to unfasten his kidskin trews. A wry smile flickered over his lips. How carefully he had dressed for this meeting, wanting to impress Juliet with his good taste. But she cared nothing for his clothes. It was his nakedness she wanted.

'Hurry now, Reynard. You keep me waiting. That is not wise. Surely you do not wish me to become angry,' Juliet said.

Her voice, the coldness of it, shocked him into action. Up until now he'd hung onto the thought that this 'lesson' was a game, something Madame had dreamt up to entertain herself. Surely it was a prank. They would all begin to laugh soon, he louder than the rest of them, and then they'd go downstairs and talk and drink fine wine.

Now he saw that he was mistaken. There was nothing of levity in any of their faces. Should he stop this? Perhaps it was already too late. The thought sent a tremor through him, though he straightened his back and squared his shoulders. As he stood before them, confident in his young strength and beauty, clothed only in spotless white linen drawers, he felt a small frisson of fear.

Juliet took one step towards him and her breasts, high and firm, moved slightly. Surely her small nipples were rouged. They were very red and seemed to invite his touch. How tiny her waist looked, entrapped as it was by the black velvet corset. Fine black satin straps encircled the garment, each of them fastened by a buckle of carved jet.

She bent towards him and gave him a cold smile.

'Did you not understand? I asked you to disrobe fully. Why are you still wearing your drawers?'

This was ridiculous. He would not be ordered about like this. Reynard straightened to his full height and stared down at her. Juliet's veiled, grey eyes met his, fearlessly. He was disconcerted. No woman had ever challenged him like this.

There was the whisper of cloth brushing against skin as Juliet adjusted her position, moving even closer. Her mouth pursed with displeasure. Reynard heard the sound before he realised what it was.

Juliet had snapped the tip of the crop she held across her outstretched palm. That smart little slap of leather against skin held menace and something else – a promise?

'I won't have disobedience, but I can see that you need to learn it,' she said softly, almost gently. 'Your first lesson will be the most difficult. For you, not for me.' And there was a flash of wicked humour about her mouth now.

'Now wait just a – ' Reynard began, his voice tailing off as Madame and Estelle appeared at his side.

'I thought you understood, monsieur,' Madame said. 'Did you not agree to take part in our lessons? Indeed you were eager to do so. Surely I remember that you gave your word or am I mistaken?'

'Yes. I did. But I – '

'Then the matter is simple. Black and white, not open to discussion. Make up your mind, monsieur. You will do as Juliet wishes: obey her every command and put yourself completely at her mercy –

or you will leave this room and my Academy and never return. Is that so difficult to understand?'

'No. No it's not,' Reynard managed to get out through dry lips.

'Bon. The choice is yours, monsieur. We await your decision.'

Reynard looked from one to the other. Madame was perfectly calm as usual, her pale face set in the expression of severity which he recognised. Estelle looked a little nervous, but excited. Her eyes slid from Madame's face to Juliet's, but she did not meet his eye.

Both women wore dark breeches and fine, white silk shirts. He could detect the shape of their breasts through the fabric and see their nipples. Madame's were dark and well-defined in shape, while Estelle's were paler, almost merging with her skin.

Only Juliet had her breasts bared and, as she shifted position, Reynard saw with delight that she was naked under the looped up full skirt. The line of her hip and the full globes of her buttocks were visible through the white fabric. If the skirt was not so bunched into folds at the front, he might have been able to see the dark curls that clustered around her sex. He knew that her maiden hair would be dark and abundant, a frame for the musky, scented folds he so loved on a woman.

He couldn't take his eyes from her. She was perfection, all he'd ever dreamed of.

Juliet stood waiting patiently, one hand outstretched palm upwards, the riding crop bouncing gently up and down. When she saw that his attention had centred on the crop, she began to slap the notched tip more forcefully against her hand.

This time, the slight sound of it, the whisper of leather against flesh, went through him like a blade. It was impossible to leave now. He couldn't bear to be excluded from the Academy, from the strange erotic lessons, from the company of the most exciting, cultured women he had ever met.

'I will stay, Madame,' he said, and was shocked to hear his voice. How desperate he sounded.

'Then follow me,' Juliet said without preamble. 'And let us have no more argument. No, don't hesitate. Leave your drawers on for the moment.'

Reynard's breath left him in a long sigh. It seemed that he had gained some kind of a respite. His decision was made and there was a kind of relief in that. It was as if he was free to participate fully and all his senses seemed to awake at once. Every detail of this experience would be forever imprinted on his consciousness. Indeed, he wanted to savour it, to make it into something tangible, like a dark jewel.

The polished floor boards were cold and smooth against the soles of his feet as he crossed the room. Light streamed in the floor-length windows, giving a stark beauty to the almost empty dance studio. The white walls, the shapes of flowers and fruits on the railing that encircled the room and the honey-coloured floor, gave the room a stylised elegance.

Reynard was entranced by the surroundings and by the presence of the three women, each of them absolutely suited to the position they occupied.

Juliet paused next to the heavy wrought-iron table. Picking up the white vase she upturned it slowly. Water and flowers poured onto the marble table top. Long stemmed arum lilies were strewn in disarray across the black marble, their greenish-white trumpets looking tender and lovely against the shiny surface. The sound of water dripping, echoed loudly in the bare room.

Juliet's actions were unexpected; perhaps in any other situation they would have been common-place, but they affected Reynard immediately. For some reason he found the spectacle of the spilled flowers almost unbearably erotic. He moved his hands to cover himself, knowing that his cock was rigid and pushing against the buttoned front of his drawers.

Juliet laughed softly, her voice husky. And Reynard's face grew hot with shame. She hadn't even touched him and here he was as tumescent as a love-sick adolescent. He was at a loss to understand himself. The tension within the room, the silent appraisal of the three woman, threw him into a state of heightened arousal. For the first time in his life he feared that he'd ejaculate if they so much as touched him.

He clenched his teeth against that awful possibility and tried to control his emotions.

Juliet gestured to him to move closer. He watched the movement of her slim white hand in silent, almost horrified fascination. His legs moved of their own volition, until he was standing next to the table.

On Juliet's order he pressed his stomach to the edge of the marble slab. Water soaked the front of his drawers and he knew that they had become transparent. Juliet could see every detail of his rigid cock. Oh God, he could feel how the wet fabric clung to his swollen glans and brushed against his cock-stem when he moved. The cluster of dark reddish hair at his groin and his tight balls must be visible too.

'No. Don't cover yourself with your hands,' Juliet said. 'I want to look at you. Turn around and face me.'

Reynard did so with reluctance, refusing to meet her eyes. Now the water soaked the back of his drawers. He felt it running down his buttocks.

'Better,' Juliet said. 'You learn obedience fast. Turn and bend over the table. Press yourself against the marble. Face down now.'

Reynard positioned himself. His skin shrank from contact with the cold marble, but he forced himself to comply. Should he sweep the marble clear of flowers and water? Juliet had not ordered him to do so. He lowered his upper body to the table top, crushing the lilies beneath him. He felt their cool petals against his body and face. The fresh green scent of them filled his mouth and nose.

The sheen of water was slippery at first, but it diminished rapidly as it soaked into his drawers. Reynard gripped the edge of the table top, shivering and flexing his buttocks against the now sodden fabric. The coldness of the marble ought to have calmed his ardour but, perversely, it seemed only to strengthen it. His cock was hot and throbbing, pressing into his belly as he lay stretched out.

He couldn't see Juliet now, but he heard the whisper of her skirt train on the bare boards. Estelle laughed softly and Madame said something in a quiet voice.

Reynard waited in an agony of apprehension. Was this to be the extent of his humiliation? Perhaps they were only playing with him. He felt a thrill of disappointment. If they dismissed him now, he might beg to be allowed to stay. Oh God. What was happening to him?

'I'm going to punish you a little for your disobedience,' Juliet said coolly. 'As this is your first time I'll be merciful.'

Something within Reynard soared. His 'first time', then there would be others? That thought blocked out all else.

When the crop descended, crashing down across his buttocks, he cried out. The pain was worse than anything he'd ever imagined. For a second it blocked out everything, then warmth rushed to fill the place of the soreness.

A moment's respite, then the next blow bisected the first. Reynard clenched his hands into fists, crushing one of the lilies between his fingers until the sticky sap trickled down his hand.

Ah God, he'd never felt anything like this. He couldn't stand it. He should move, protest, but he did nothing. Another blow slashed down onto the wet stretched fabric across his buttocks. A sob rose in his throat, but he bit it back.

Juliet was cruel and heartless. He hated her. He worshipped her. Tears burned his eyes as he screwed his face into a rictus of agony.

Yet, there was a dimension beyond the pain. It was fading even now. The blows had ceased. Perhaps his tormentor judged that he'd had enough for now. His buttocks flamed and throbbed, finding an echo in the rigid flesh of his cock which pressed against the marble.

Now hands took hold of his buttocks, stroking

gently, assessing the level of heat and soreness and sending little shocks of sensation to his every nerve end. Incredibly his cock leapt in response. As he twisted he felt the slippery fluid that wept from the little cock-mouth.

He knew that they were Juliet's long white fingers that stroked him, that were even now feeling under him and squeezing his cock-stem. He gave her his pain and arousal as a gift.

A unique sense of longing woke in Reynard. Yes. Oh, yes. Let this go on. Let her do as she wished with him. He didn't care what she did, as long as she just kept doing it. He was her slave.

In the midst of his discomfort and confusion, he had found a small, calm place within himself. He knew with blinding certainty, that this was what he wanted, had always wanted, but never found.

Juliet was the women he'd been seeking. She had somehow seen through his outer persona to the secrets within. He felt such a rush of emotion that another sob lodged in his throat and emerged as a sort of strangled plea.

'Juliet,' he whispered.

He seemed never to have been truly alive until this moment. Her slim fingers were stroking him to a pitch of pleasure he had not deemed possible. The throbbing in his buttocks matched the pulsings in his cock, the sensation building, building . . .

Then she stopped her manipulation and he felt utterly desolate. Losing all pride, he begged her to continue.

'Please. Oh God. Juliet. Please . . . Don't stop.'

He'd been so near. But she was cruel, so wonder-

fully cruel that he didn't mind waiting for the
release that must surely come.

The hand that stroked across his burning buttocks was gentle now. A simple gesture, but he felt
a rush of gratitude towards her.

'Patience,' she said softly. 'This is only the beginning. Pleasure should be anticipated.'

The beginning. How wonderful that sounded.
He'd do whatever she wanted, kiss her feet, give
her the world – if only she'd consent to pledge
herself to him.

He knew he was raving, but he didn't care. He'd
never felt so desperate for anything in his entire
life.

'Get up now, Reynard,' Juliet said coldly. 'Your
punishment is over – for the moment. I would test
your obedience now. I want you to show me how
well you can pleasure a woman.'

Reynard pushed against the sides of the table,
lifting his belly off the wet marble. He'd give Juliet
more pleasure than she'd dreamed possible.

Juliet watched Reynard ease himself upright.

Her hands were trembling so much that she hid
them in the folds of her full white skirt. She'd been
right about him, but his response to her, to the
humiliation, had exceeded even her expectations.

He was certainly beautiful. His body was flaw-
less, less heavily muscled than Etienne or Andreas,
but well formed nonetheless. His dark red hair had
come loose from its binding at its nape. Thick
strands of it fell either side of his face and trailed
onto his broad shoulders.

She felt tenderness for him at that moment. For

although she sensed his utter capitulation to her will, he held himself erect and retained a certain pride. Even the sodden drawers could not demean him completely. They clung to his bulging thighs and slim hips, outlining his cock which jutted out potently as he stood up straight.

Desire for him centred in the pit of her belly. Her sex-lips felt heavy and moist.

'Turn around,' she ordered.

And when he did, she saw how his buttocks glowed through the wet linen.

'Take off your drawers,' she said.

Reynard complied, stripping the clinging drawers down his legs and stepping out of them. She examined the marks she'd made and saw Madame flash her a glance of approval. The weals were placed regularly, covering the swell of his taut buttocks but not encroaching on the skin of his back or thighs. Each thin, red line was stark and raised against the pale flesh.

'Well done,' Madame said. 'He'll wear the badge of your caresses for some time. Shall we continue?'

Juliet saw how Reynard's mouth trembled as he met her eye. He's mad for me, she thought, enjoying the feeling of having power over him. Oh, this was such a well-defined pleasure. It was like a drug. A drug she wanted more of. Now she'd test how far Reynard would go to please her.

Juliet caught Estelle's eye and smiled meaningfully at her friend. Estelle understood at once and smiled back. She nodded.

'Over here?' she asked Juliet.

Juliet nodded.

'Go along, Reynard. You're to follow Estelle.'

She saw a brief look of puzzlement pass over Reynard's face. It was the first time that Estelle had taken an active part in the lesson. He'd thought she was only an observer.

Estelle paused with her back to the wrought-iron wall barre. Leaning back on her elbows, so that her lower body was thrust out a little, she placed her feet apart and waited for Reynard to approach.

Juliet and Madame stood either side of Estelle. Juliet fixed Reynard with a haughty stare.

'On your knees,' she ordered. 'I want to see how well trained you are becoming.'

He looked askance at her.

'But I thought – '

She gave a dismissive little laugh.

'You thought you'd be pleasuring me? Oh dear. You didn't really think that I'd allow that did you? It's far too soon. You're new and untried as yet. You have to earn special privileges I'm afraid.'

Reynard hung his head.

'I see . . . What must I do?'

'I didn't tell you to speak,' Juliet rapped. 'But I'll overlook that on this occasion. Unbutton Estelle's shirt and unfasten her breeches.'

Estelle closed her eyes as Reynard did as Juliet ordered. Her lips were parted slightly, showing her uneven white teeth. Reynard pushed the shirt off Estelle's shoulders. It slipped down her arms with a whisper and bunched against her wrists, lodging in a rumpled cloud against the iron barre. She made no move to shrug it off.

Estelle's slim torso was revealed. Her rounded breasts, surprisingly large and with soft pale nipples, hung a little to each side under their own weight. Her ribcage was delicate and sloped down to her softly rounded belly.

Juliet looked at her friend's body with approval. The shy reticent Estelle seemed transformed at this moment. She looked young and very appealing with her face softened by desire.

Reynard eased the black breeches down over Estelle's hips and thighs, his gaze lingering on her pubic mound. He then knelt to unlace her knee-length boots.

Juliet watched in silence, now and then meeting Madame's eye. She could sense Madame's pleasure and pride in her pupils' prowess. After the interlude in the orangery, she could also tell that Madame was excited but well in control of her emotions.

There came the muffled sound of Estelle's boots hitting the wooden floor. The black trews followed them and Estelle was naked. Reynard stood up.

'Is Estelle not beautiful?' Juliet asked Reynard. 'Look at her face. She wants you. It is a privilege to pleasure her. You may begin. See that you give a good account of yourself – otherwise I might have to chastise you again.'

Reynard looked unsure of himself. She smiled inwardly. No doubt he considered himself to be an excellent lover; most men did, according to Madame. He had a reputation as a rake, so would have loved many women. But she doubted whether he'd ever pleasured a woman while others looked on and judged his performance.

His tumescence had subsided somewhat.

'Is this reticence, monsieur? Surely not. I expect obedience.'

She reached out and placed her hand on his belly.
The muscles were hard and ridged under her palm.
Sliding her hand down, she encircled his cock-stem
and worked the loose skin back and forth until he
was breathing unevenly.

Reynard swayed towards her. She laughed and
removed her hand. Now his cock stood out as
firmly as before.

'It isn't me you have to please,' she said. 'Estelle
is waiting. See how white and slim her thighs are.
Don't you long to part them and caress her sex?'

Reynard turned towards Estelle, trying to conceal
his reluctance. Plainly it was Juliet he wanted, but
as he looked at Estelle's firm young body, Juliet
saw his reticence fade.

Estelle shifted slightly and flexed her knees so
that the lips of her parted sex were visible. The
inner folds were pale and smooth – more peach
than pink, tender and new looking. Drops of moisture glistened on the few silky hairs that covered
her mound.

Juliet smiled. So little Estelle had become aroused
by watching her beat Reynard. How could Reynard
resist that girlish little sex? How could anyone? She
felt herself growing more aroused as Estelle arched
her back and pushed the hungry little nether-mouth
towards Reynard.

Reynard bent and dropped a kiss on Estelle's
belly, before kneeling between her thighs. Reaching
out he parted the flesh-lips and pressed them gently
backwards, the motion causing Estelle's swollen
little bud to stand proud of the surrounding folds.

Pressing gently on the pleasure bud with the tip
of one finger, Reynard smoothed the little bud of

flesh up towards Estelle's belly. Estelle moaned and writhed as he stimulated the sensitive morsel.

Juliet watched the strong slope of Reynard's back and his narrow hips as he leant forward and began to tongue Estelle's wet sex. He moved his head back and forth as he penetrated her with the tip of his tongue and then slid his mouth up and down the slippery folds.

Estelle threw her head back and slumped down onto her elbows. Her thighs trembled as Reynard lifted them and set them onto his shoulders. He moved his head slowly, his whole mouth fastened to Estelle's sex in an erotic kiss. Little cries escaped the young woman as she reached her climax.

Juliet was tempted to order Reynard to pleasure her in the same way, but she knew that she had to keep him waiting. That way, he would remain hungry for her, desperate for the easement that only she could give him.

Estelle moaned when Reynard stood up and swung her hips up towards his straining member. Reaching his hands under her bottom to support her, he settled her long legs around his waist.

Estelle linked her ankles together as Reynard pressed his cock-tip to the entrance between her flesh-lips. Turning his head, Reynard met Juliet's eyes. He held her gaze while he pressed forward and buried his full length inside Estelle.

At Estelle's long sigh of pleasure, Juliet's womb contracted. Her own sex felt heavy and swollen, the creamy moisture oozing from the closed slit. She squeezed her thighs together, but the compression only made her feel more aroused. Later, in the dark solitude on her curtained bed, she would have to ease herself.

Madame's black eyes were sparkling and her little red mouth was pursed in a wicked smile. She knows exactly how I feel, thought Juliet. She flashed Madame a rueful grin. This lesson was for Reynard's benefit, not for her own. But it would pay dividends for the future.

'Restraint is a difficult lesson to learn,' Madame said softly for Juliet's ears alone. 'You are doing very well. Those who would wield power must bury their own desires until the time is right. When you inspire devotion in others, Juliet, you must be worthy of receiving it.'

Madame gave a husky little laugh as Reynard threw back his hair, shaking the sweat-darkened strands from his eyes. His face was screwed into an expression of the most exquisite pleasure.

'Look at him. I never saw a more willing subject. He's almost entirely yours already. If you want him, that is.'

Juliet nodded.

'I know,' she said. 'And I do want him. He's perfect for me. I'll not find another so well suited for my purpose. Papa will be overjoyed.'

A particularly loud moan from Estelle dragged Juliet's attention back to the two figures. Reynard's buttocks clenched as he thrust powerfully into Estelle. She dug her heels into his back, urging him to greater efforts. The muscles of Reynard's arms and legs were corded with the sexual tension that bound him.

Throwing back his head, Reynard clenched his teeth, his thrusts becoming more frenzied. In a moment he would climax. It was time for Juliet to let him know that the moment was hers.

Stepping to one side of him, she meshed her fingers in his long hair and dragged his head round so that he faced her. She smelt his expensive cologne and the sharper tang of his sweat. From the slippery joined bodies, arose the smell of musk and salt.

Their eyes met. In Reynard's she saw adoration, but it was mixed with anger. Good. He still fought himself, even while he acknowledged that she held dominance over him.

Ah, theirs would be a joining of fire and ice. Wholly exciting and satisfying to them both.

Reynard licked his dry lips, his expression pleading now as he pulled his cock almost all the way out of Estelle's body and rimmed the tight little entrance.

'God, Juliet . . .' he murmured.

She knew that he was aching for her kiss. Tremors rippled down his thighs as he tried to hold back his climax. She saw the need in his eyes for some gesture of affection, however slight.

Juliet sensed what she must do. Smiling narrowly, she bent close and allowed her mouth to brush against his in the merest whisper of a kiss. He strained towards her, desperate for a more prolonged contact.

Laughing softly she moved away a fraction, so that her lips left his but her breath played over his mouth. With the point of her tongue she tasted his lips. They were warm and salty with sweat. Reynard made a sound deep in his throat and thrust his head towards her, grinding his mouth down onto hers. Juliet smiled.

Swinging back her free hand she brought it crashing down on his abused buttocks.

Reynard screamed with the unexpected pain and surged forward, burying his cock to the hilt inside Estelle and grinding his pubis against hers. Estelle moaned and surged forward to meet the fresh onslaught. She bucked and writhed under him, then emitted high little screams as her second climax coursed through her. Her back arched as she lifted herself clear of the wrought-iron rail.

Reynard sobbed, his face screwed into a rictus of pleasure-pain, as Juliet spanked him soundly. Beside himself now and aching for release, he thrust back and forth, his emerging cock-stem so engorged that it looked red-purple.

'I want to see you climax. Pull out of her,' Juliet ordered.

And Reynard did, collapsing onto Estelle's belly as his whole body spasmed. The sperm jetted across Estelle's taut flesh in great tearing spurts. Shuddering, his shoulders wracked by an excess of emotion, he clung to Estelle's slim body, his arms wrapped tightly around her waist.

But the name he whispered through clenched teeth was Juliet's.

Juliet felt a profound sense of completion. He was hers now, totally. Even if he took another woman, it would be *her* face her saw, *her* kisses he tasted. Controlling the desire that seemed to hold her whole body in its grip, she ran her stinging palm down one cool thigh, loving the contrast of temperatures.

The erotic tension had left her exhausted. If she didn't obtain some relief soon, she'd go mad. Madame caught her eye and Juliet knew that she need not burn for much longer. Suddenly eager for the dark pleasure which only Madame could supply, Juliet decided to bring the lesson to an abrupt close.

'Loose Estelle, Reynard,' she ordered, 'and clean that mess from her stomach. No. Not with a cloth. Use your mouth.'

Reynard complied at once. Estelle stood, arms at her sides, while Reynard licked the creamy sperm from her belly. She smoothed the damp hair back from his forehead and he flashed her an absent smile, his whole body attuned for Juliet's voice, Juliet's caress.

Ignoring Reynard, who remained kneeling on the polished wooden floor, Juliet took Estelle in her arms. After kissing her friend's cheek tenderly, she gathered up her clothes and handed them to her.

Estelle dressed swiftly, shrugging the shirt over her shoulders and belting the breeches. She pulled on her boots and held her foot out to Reynard who rested the sole of her boot on his knee. Deftly he laced the boot.

'Remain as you are until we have gone,' Juliet said to Reynard. 'Then you may dress and leave.'

Without a backward glance, she linked arms with Estelle and walked towards the door, the train of her full white skirt brushing the floor boards.

Reynard watched her, his eyes filled with a mixture of longing and self disgust. How could Juliet dismiss him like this? She preferred Estelle as an escort. Even now he could go after her, drag her back into the room and force her to pleasure him. She looked beautiful and arrogant in the velvet corset, her long pale limbs showing faintly through the white skirt.

He cursed under his breath and made a movement to get to his feet, then thought better of it. Juliet heard the movement. She paused and looked back at him.

'You seem confused, monsieur,' she said in a severe tone. 'The lesson is over. What more did you expect?'

His handsome face was swollen and tear-streaked. He looked like a Botticelli angel, pale and graceful against the honey-coloured floor. The contrast of his strength of body and emotional frailty sent a thrill to Juliet's loins.

'More . . .' Reynard whispered. 'Just – more . . .'

She almost went to him, but saw Madame shake her head. Madame was right of course. It would not do to show pity to him now. And whatever his demeanour at present, he did not really expect or desire it.

The three women walked to the door. Estelle disappeared first. Madame and Juliet stood side by side. Unseen by Reynard, Madame slipped her hand up Juliet's back and began caressing the exposed nape of her neck.

Juliet could not suppress a shiver of eagerness. The inheld arousal churned within her. Her nipples were hard and aching.

'This lesson is at an end. There is nothing else to say,' Madame said impatiently. 'Come Juliet.'

'Please. When . . .' Reynard faltered.

196

Madame turned, smiling with perfect understanding. 'You are Juliet's now. Ask her.'

Reynard clenched his fists and turned brimming eyes on Juliet.

She made her voice level, though Madame's strong fingers on her neck were maddening.

'When I wish, Reynard. And not before. You will await my summons.'

Turning on her heel, she left the room. Part of her exhulted. It was as Madame said. He was truly hers. Mere formalities would be necessary now. Legal documents and a ring. But he would never belong to her more than he did at this moment.

Yes. She had Reynard.

But was he enough?

A Brush With
Officer Schroeder

Portia Da Costa

The last of our three short stories is by Portia Da Costa whose name should be familiar to regular Black Lace readers. A prolific author, she has written four books for the Black Lace series. They are: *Gemini Heat*, *The Tutor*, *The Devil Inside* and *Gothic Blue*. She specialises in contemporary settings with a fetishistic twist.

There's just something intriguing about traffic cops. *A Brush With Officer Schroeder* is written specially for readers who like a man in a uniform. When Lise-Anne gets pulled for speeding by Officer Schroeder, the terms of her fine are open to negotiation in the most creative ways.

A Brush With Officer Schroeder

*T*he only problem with having a big, fast car is that big, fast bike-cops tend to chase them.

My car is bigger and faster than most, and as I was also doing at least thirty over the limit, I wasn't surprised to find a cop on my tail!

Not that I didn't deserve to be pulled over. I love speed, I really get off on it; and when you combine fast driving with personal power, then throw in a pinch of pure devilment for good measure, you end up with one hell of a potent, self-sustaining aphrodisiac.

On the fateful day in question, I was racing towards a deal that would bring me more power than I'd ever dreamt of, at a speed that had me excited anyway, so I was just about as turned on as it was possible to be outside a bedroom. I was sorely tempted to pull over and do something about that feeling – but I knew I just didn't have the time to make the best of it.

Something else I didn't have time for was a certain familiar, oscillating wail, and the sleek, almost bullet-like shape that loomed in the dead centre of my rear-view mirror. I didn't have time for much more than anything but getting to my meeting, but as a dark, dark shadow reeled in the distance between us, I knew I was going to have to *make* time.

I'd never crossed swords with a member of the newly formed Pan-State Patrol before, but it wasn't difficult to deduce what he would be like. Our nation's bike cops are one of the last bastions of male chauvinism; a force of archetypally hard-nosed policemen who really get off on laying down the law to speeding women. Especially well-dressed, successful, blonde women like me. And for my part, I'm even more of a target for these turbo-charged Neanderthals than most women, because I have the effrontery to like my own sex just as much as I like men.

It works both ways, though, because I also happen to like cops just as much as I like girls. There's something quite irresistible about an implacable, dark-clad law defender with a hunk of high energy brute power between his legs. And the motorbikes themselves are pretty sexy too!

Unfortunately for me, the super-tuned bikes that the Pan-State Patrol ride can out-accelerate all but the very fastest cars, so it was pointless me even thinking of trying to lose him. Torn between cheering and weeping, I pulled over on to the side of the road and wondered whether to sit tight or to get out and face the music.

Get out, I decided, and get out immediately. My

cop had already cruised to a halt, leapt off his machine and was marching down the blacktop towards me. In total confusion, I watched him bearing down on me. The clock was ticking on my deal, yet I was dying to see this unknown cop up close.

He was not the tallest patrolman I had ever seen, or – given the thickness of the grotesquely macho leather uniform he was wearing – the broadest. In fact, he was probably fairly lean beneath that reinforced suit. It could be quite bleak out on the exposed freeway sometimes, and he would need something pretty substantial to protect him at the bone-chilling speeds he and his brethren seemed to favour.

His long, super-confident stride filled me with a wild mix of emotions: anger, fear and an acute and very tangible arousal. Skinny cops are notoriously the meanest, and while I'm attracted to women as blonde and feminine as I am, I much prefer my menfolk dark and moody. The approaching cop looked very dark, and his smooth, brutal athleticism made my already moist sex tighten in excitement.

'May I see your ID, ma'am?' His voice was gruff but lightish, sensual in a way that only made things worse. His stance was menacing yet relaxed, and promised viper-like speed if I should even think of making a break for it. I handed him my company ID card – which I had had the foresight to get out in readiness – and he seemed to study it as if it revealed my every secret.

'Lise-Anne Lineweaver, resident of Chicago, born 1970, height five six and a half, hair blonde, eyes green-hazel – ' He paused in his listing of my attributes, and though I was not able to see his eyes beneath his visor, I knew he was cataloguing my other – unlisted – statistics: measurements, thirty-seven, twenty-four, thirty-five: weight, 119 pounds, perfectly distributed; star sign, Gemini; erotic preference, most decidedly bisexual. Was he impressed? Was he even interested? Or was he just an iron-clad lawman bereft of feelings or sensitivity? At the risk of being immodest, I decided I was slipping. Men were usually coming on to me by now. Women too. And in this case I really needed to impress. If I missed that meeting, I could forget my crucial deal, and maybe even the whole of my career.

'Is there a problem, officer?' I tried to play it cool, even though I was burning up. I'm crazy, I know, but add danger and conflict to that mixture of speed, power and sex – and I'm anybody's. My libido overrides my self-control.

'Yes, ma'am, I'd call forty over the legal limit a problem,' he intoned solemnly. 'A pretty serious one. Is your speedometer functioning correctly?'

'Er, yes, Officer, Officer-' I checked out the single name on the breast-pocket of his chunky leathers. 'Yes, Officer Schroeder, I'm afraid it is. I know I shouldn't have been going so fast, but I'm due at an important meeting soon. There's a lot riding on it, officer. Under normal circumstances, I wouldn't dream of exceeding the limit.'

'That's as maybe, ma'am,' Officer Schroeder went on, unperturbed, 'but I'm afraid it is my duty to book you.'

I shivered. It was bleak out there in the middle

of nowhere, and while Schroeder was snugly encased in leather, boots, gloves and helmet, my own outfit – high heels and a thin silk suit with just a few scraps of lace beneath it – was far from adequate for the conditions.

'You cold, Ms Lineweaver?' he asked abruptly, and I nodded and shivered again for effect. 'We'd better discuss this inside the vehicle then.' He nodded in the direction of the beast that had caused all the trouble.

I shivered yet again, as he opened the rear passenger door, but this time it wasn't due to any chilly breezes.

Was I imagining things or had he laid a special emphasis on the word 'discuss'? And why the back seat, when the glove compartment – and the rest of my documents – were in the front? As the door clicked shut behind him, and he settled his lean, black-leather-clad body into the back seat, I felt a tremor of anticipation take me. A frisson that Schroeder could not possibly have detected unless he had X-ray vision and was able to see right through my clothing to my sex.

In the enclosed space he was even more imposing; bulkier yet, paradoxically, more elegant. He stretched his long legs out in front of him, his pose masterful yet not exactly what I would have called policeman-like. And worse, and even less cop-like, he stayed silent for one long full minute as – presumably – he perused me through the blackness of his visor.

Without speaking a word he seemed to intimidate and give orders; though to do what, I hardly dared contemplate. My crazed imagination and my mad, bad body kept telling me it was something sexual, but with his intentions masked – both by his visor and by his stout leather biking trousers, which were no doubt lined with body armour – my more rational side had no way of knowing.

He had pinned me with a gaze I couldn't see, but I was so excited that I couldn't keep my body still. It was like being ogled by Darth Vader, and my black-clad cop was every bit as sexy as the Dark Lord of the Sith.

I jumped a mile when he flipped up the visor; but then gasped with disappointment. He wore shades beneath it. Why the hell did bike cops always feel they had to conform to their stereotype? Even though I actually adore that stereotype, I would have preferred to see his eyes. Denied the privilege, I decided they were blue. Very blue. And very very cold.

As I shifted my thighs, worried about the state of my underwear, he shifted his. Cutting some slack for his erection perhaps? We were here, in this enclosed area, hidden from prying eyes, to discuss the exceeding of limits; but suddenly vehicle speed didn't seem to be the issue.

'Something bothering you, ma'am?' he enquired, his tongue flicking out momentarily to lick his lips. The tiny gesture left moisture behind, a gleam that hit me like lightning. A flash of heat went straight to my vulva and my hips bumped of their own accord. Oh God, that mouth of his! It was the only one of his erogenous zones I could see but it was enough. His lips were firm and very hard-looking, yet the lower one was full and succulent. I imagined biting into it, in the heat of passion, as he fucked me.

'Do you have a problem, ma'am?' He was so smooth, so cool, so self-aware.

The bastard! I don't know how he knew, but he did. Maybe he really did have X-ray vision, and had seen what was happening between my legs, seen the state that his dark authority, and my own confusion had brought me to. I fought the urge to press my hand to my aching clit, and flicked a look at the small, very expensive overnight case that he had moved along the seat and placed between us. I'd been planning a stopover when my meeting had ended, to celebrate, and my case contained assorted toiletries, clean panties, and my lucky silver-backed hair brush. As well as using this to tame my tousled locks I sometimes used it for a rather different purpose, which was also, I suppose, a form of taming – and dear God, how I needed it now!

'Open the case, ma'am,' Schroeder instructed. Technically, the order was routine – the standard check for firearms or narcotics – but I had a deep, purely visceral feeling that he wasn't really interested in illegal items at all. He just wanted to see my most intimate possessions.

Obediently I clicked the catch and opened the lid, glancing first at the panties and brush and then back at Schroeder. God damn the son of a bitch, why wouldn't he let me see his eyes? Why wouldn't he even give me a chance to believe we could do a deal?

Quickly and efficiently, he rifled through the case's few contents, making me shudder when he lifted the panties, unfolded them and almost – just almost – seemed to study the crotch. My dewy, aroused vulva moistened further as he ran his fingers assessingly over the brush's rigid handle.

'You use this a lot, ma'am?' His voice was neutral; music to my hopeful ears, yet still entirely unrevealing. Did he know what I used that brush for? A woman would have picked up on it straight away, and I realised, as he twisted the handle caressingly between his finger and thumb, that Schroeder had sussed my secret too. Silver looked as good against tough black leather as it did against soft pink juiciness, and that thoughtfully shaped handle was just too evocative to pass over.

I nodded dumbly.

'Care to show me how, ma'am?'

The moment of unthinkable truth had arrived, but this request for a lewd act felt strangely comfortable. It felt like fate, like destiny almost, but a token protest of outraged innocence still seemed necessary.

'I – I – I don't – I can't. . .'

'As you wish, ma'am,' Schroeder replied, apparently unconcernd as he reached for the door handle. 'I'll just take the keys to the vehicle, then I'll call a squad car to take you in to the nearest town.'

'But, officer! My meeting!'

Without a word he named his price, his helmeted head inclining minutely.

'How?' I queried through parched lips.

'What you usually do would be just fine, ma'am,' he said softly, and settled himself deeper into the seat.

Damn those stupid reinforced trousers! It wasn't

fair! I couldn't see what sort of an effect I was having on him – but he would soon see the effect he had on me. I felt so mixed up. Half of me wanted him to unfasten his zipper and share this thing with me; yet by the same token, it seemed gross, somehow, to disturb that perfect leather smoothness.

But I hadn't any time for debate. I was in a hurry. And not just to get to the meeting I had told him about.

Avoiding the stare I could not see, I unbuttoned the jacket of my thin suit.

'Nice brassiere, ma'am,' commented Schroeder conversationally as my fingers went to the clip between my breasts. I felt both ashamed and proud; my nipples looked so hard and red as they sprang free of their black lace enclosure. I took one between each finger and thumb, then tugged in a way that made my clitoris itch like fury. Schroeder just watched me, one hand resting loosely in the region of his groin, the other tapping my brush against his thigh.

I twisted my nipples – roughly, this way and that – revelling in the slight pain as I pinched them in between my fingers, and in the corresponding pleasure I felt between my legs. But Schroeder appeared to be staring at my crotch, now, and I knew I had better get on with it. Hitching my floaty skirt up to my waist, I hesitated, then pulled my panties down to my ankles. The black silk had a big damp patch on it; a sight that, to my surprise, pleased me considerably.

I needed the brush now, and like the mind-reader I was beginning to believe he was, Schroeder passed it to me. I was disappointed when our fingers didn't touch.

I paused again at that point, and he nodded. With a deep sigh, a mixture of relief and mortification, I pushed the silver handle into my moist and silky channel. It went in easily, even though that handle was hard and very thick. I'd never been wetter in my whole life. I closed my eyes, imagined that my brush was the dark god Schroeder, and proceeded to fuck it as if the world was about to end. Shoving with one hand, feeling the bristles stabbing my fingers, I groped blindly for my clitoris with the other. Found it. Pinched it. Pinched the tiny rose-red focus of my pleasure with all the force and savagery I had previously used on my nipples.

I was coming in seconds. Too soon! The last functioning fragment of my brain seemed to scream. My hips bounced, my inner muscles tightened, then began to undulate around the handle, yet as I rode the sensations like the man's own motorcycle, an inner voice insisted I had cheated Schroeder.

Suddenly, the rest of my mind meshed shockingly with that small grain of reason. The brush was being pulled out of me – but not by my own hand. I looked down and saw leather-covered fingers drawing the slick, wet silver away from my flesh, breaking the glittering thread of juice that joined it to my body.

'Nice brush,' he observed, tossing it into my case, 'Maybe I'll get one myself.'

What? Still dazed and splay-legged, I watched him open the door and climb nimbly from the car. The cool air made my pussy tingle as he gave me a salute and what just might have been an admiring smile.

'You can go now, Ms Lineweaver, but keep the speed down.' He turned smartly and walked away towards his bike. 'Have a nice day!' he tossed over his shoulder as I adjusted my skirt, my bra and my top, then scrambled out of the car myself and climbed pantie-less into the front seat.

My meeting seemed oddly unimportant now, but nevertheless as I started the engine and checked my watch, I saw that I'd still got a good hour in hand.

I should have moved off then, but instead I just stared at the rear-view mirror. Schroeder was a God damn pervert, but there was something about him that made it quite impossible to let go.

As the minutes ticked by, my eyes were riveted to Schroeder's slim dark figure. I watched, rapt, as he put up his leather-covered hands and – at last – unfastened his menacing helmet.

I think I forgot to breathe then. My life turned inside out as Schroeder lifted away the shiny, polished 'lid' and released a great cascade of lush, silvery platinum hair; a shimmering fall far blonder, far softer and far fluffier than mine was. It streamed all the way down over those intimidating jacketed shoulders and way beyond them.

With a sharp gasp, I took in breath, then held it again as Schroeder dispensed with his gloves and helmet, then shrugged off that boxy leather jacket – a carapace, I realised, that had been covering a body of exquisitely delicate charm. Not to mention a trim, rounded bosom graced by a black lace underwired bra, almost exactly like the one I wore myself.

Grinning wickedly, Schroeder then removed the shades that had so defied me, and began walking in my direction, making it easier and easier for me to see a pair of eyes that were every bit as blue as I had dreamt they would be.

True blue. Ice-blue. Ice-baby-blue eyes that seemed to impale me as they got nearer and nearer.

'What time's that meeting, Ms Lineweaver?' Schroeder enquired suavely as – like a mindless sex zombie – I climbed into the back seat again beside her.

'T – two pm,' I stammered, watching her work on her cumbersome buckled belt.

'No problem. You'll make it.' The belt dropped away. 'With a police escort.'

Long, slender fingers dealt effortlessly with the heavy duty zipper, the leather fly, the protective Kevlar, and then with the scrap of sheer black silk that lay beneath it all.

'OK then, ma'am, let's take a spin with that brush of yours, shall we?'

The Stallion

Georgina Brown

The Stallion by Georgina Brown is the kind of book which immediately appeals to anyone who has read women's blockbuster stories. The world of showjumping is as steamy as it is competitive and Penny Bennett is determined to succeed in any way she can. She joins Beaumont's exclusive riding academy and gets more than she bargains for in an atmosphere of unbridled kinkiness.

The sequel to *The Stallion*, entitled *Runners and Riders*, is due for publication in October 1996. Georgina Brown has written one other Black Lace title. It is called *Eye of the Storm* and is set amongst the jet-setting yachting fraternity.

The Stallion

There were chandeliers in the dining-loom, all starlike sparkle hanging from the high ceiling, which was predominantly Wedgwood blue, but with swirls of ornamental plaster picked out in crisp gold and icy white.

The windows were like the ones Penny remembered from Alistair's office, Georgian panes set in big sash windows that left little room for walls between the high ceiling and the blue and gold plush pile carpet. The curtains were gold damask with heavy tie-backs that hooked to the unusually pronounced brass phalli of flying cherubs.

The walls that were left were white, their expansive iciness relieved only with a dado rail of crisp blue and spine of gold. Large paintings also relieved the white walls. The frames were gilt, the subjects nude figures indulging in a variety of positions with more than one partner. Yet they were not piles of Titian flesh, all white and lumpy

with small breasts and heavy hips. These were
sleek women and well-honed and -hung men.
These were today's figures, firm and supple, unin-
hibited in their pleasures and healthy in their
bodies.

The gold, the blue, the whiteness were reflected
in a myriad shades from the overhanging chandeliers and duplicated by the lead-crystal wine
glasses. Some of the glasses contained red wine,
dark as warm blood; others housed white wine, the
liquid softly golden beneath the overhanging lights.

There were four people seated at the table: Alistair, of course; another man introduced as Auberon
Harding, a fellow rider, young and good-looking;
and another man introduced as Sir Reginald Chry-
sling, who was older, but had worn well and had
an instant, if predictable old-world charm.

'Reggie,' he corrected enthusiastically, his tongue
licking over thin lips in a strong face. 'My friends
call me Reggie.'

'Pleased to meet you,' she said, and smiled
sweetly at him as he eased himself up from his
chair in an act of old-fashioned politeness whilst
she took her own seat. Old-world charm had a
certain attraction about it, but even if it hadn't, Sir
Reggie, although his hair was white, was a well-
built man who'd obviously taken care of his body,
and in his youth must have been quite something
to look at. He still was now. His nose was slightly
hooked, his eyebrows were dark and matched his
eyes. How sensuous his lips looked when they
smiled. I wonder how many other lips they have
kissed in his lifetime, Penny mused, or how many

breasts have been sucked to distraction between his neat white teeth.

Penny beamed at them all, for no matter who looked at her and what they said, tonight she was beautiful. Tongues confirmed what eyes already said. She radiated beauty and health, and with it, sexuality.

The other person at the table was a woman who Alistair introduced as his sister, Nadine. Vaguely, Penny remembered seeing her at Alistair's side in the VIP lounges at championship events.

The two women exchanged greetings.

Penny was immediately hypnotised and discomforted by this woman. Something in Nadine's manner and the cool look in her eyes seemed to flow out from her. Whatever the nature of this strange current, it made Penny's limbs feel weak and her sex pliant.

With world-weary eyes, Nadine gazed at her with a curiously enigmatic expression and a half-smile on one side of her mouth. 'I'm very pleased to meet you,' she said slowly, elbow on table, chin supported in right hand. 'Very pleased indeed.' Her voice had a lazy buzz to it, like the idle droning of bees on a summer afternoon or the faint sound of a diesel lawnmower.

It was not just Nadine's voice that was unusual. Her appearance was dramatic, if not eccentric. Her eyes were grey, her jaw strong, her cheekbones prominent. Her hair was very white and very short, just bristles over her skull. Her skin closely matched her hair. Her eyes were lined with kohl, her lids with dark-grey shadow.

Perhaps it was the shadow that fell across her

face, but Penny had the distinct expression she was being undressed with alarming familiarity by someone she had never met, but who seemed to know her and her body very well.

'Another little jumper. Well I shall soon put you through your paces, my dear, you can count on that,' said Nadine. The trace of sarcasm was drowned with a sip of wine clasped in fingers whose nails were varnished black. Plush, thick lips pursed speculatively over a black cheroot. There was an exchange of looks between brother and sister that hinted at reproach.

'Quite a good one, so I hear,' Nadine added suddenly. 'You have a good body, my dear. Fit, trim; ideal for what is expected of you.' Now her smile was very wide and very warm. With the addition of more wine, her voice was deep, yet crisp as burned toffee.

'I try to excel in everything, as much as is possible,' returned Penny, unable to hide her unease that the wandering gaze inspired in her. Nadine had watched her behind one of those mirrors. She knew it instinctively. Determinedly, she declined to blush.

As she smiled at Alistair's sister, Penny took a deep breath. Her breasts struggled against the half-open bodice. It was a provocative move, one designed to suggest that she was both knowledgeable and available.

Her eyes took note of their individual reactions. Auberon merely blushed, his eyelids fluttering like frightened butterflies.

Experience and familiarity won through. Reggie

licked his lips and made no attempt to stop his eyes from settling on her cleavage.

Alistair, she thought, looked uncomfortable. It was as though he wanted to stare at what was on offer, but didn't dare. There was an odd look in his eyes, a mix of desire and perpetual torment.

Only Nadine's gaze was steady, her lips smiling. There was absolute boldness in her look, coupled with an odd satisfaction. Her eyes narrowed through the halo of blue smoke.

Content that she had received admiration, Penny unfolded the crisp white napkin that smelt of fresh citrus and was stiff with starch.

Nadine was directly across from her. It is easy to study looks when the subject you are studying is facing you.

It was hard not to stare at Alistair's sister. Penny tried to look away, to concentrate on the meal, sip less slowly at the wine, but Nadine surprised her. It seemed quite amazing that someone with such white hair and angular features could possibly be related to Alistair.

Nadine caught her looking and raised her blonde eyebrows towards the cropped hair that shone like silver beneath the lights.

From a distance, Penny guessed, the short glossy spikes could almost be mistaken for her bare skull. Jet earrings jiggled gently in her ears when she laughed as she did now.

Sir Reggie had cracked a joke. Penny hadn't heard it, her mind too full of analysing these people, of surmising how they might fit into the overall picture of things.

So far since coming here, she'd learned little of

timetable and other more sociable interactions; except for Gregory of course. But Gregory didn't talk much – not that such a minor problem as that detracted from his magnetism one little bit.

'I hope I haven't offended you,' said Sir Reggie suddenly, shattering the beauty and sheer sexuality of her thoughts as his hand landed on hers. 'I hope you don't mind being the butt of my little joke. I didn't really mean it, you know.'

'Not at all,' she said, smiling brightly and wondering if the wine she had been drinking had affected her hearing. 'I can take a joke any time.' Then she laughed. What he'd said about her in any joke was of no interest to her; besides, she hadn't heard him.

Her attention was drawn to Nadine whose hand reached over the table. Her palm rattled the glass and silverware as she brought it down heavily on the pure whiteness of the tablecloth.

'That's it, Penny darling. Take no notice of him. I'm sure you'll be an asset round here, darling girl. My brother appreciates perfection – in everything.'

'I won't,' she replied, her eyes catlike; her lips, glistening with the dark rich colour, slowly sipped her wine.

Their eyes met as Nadine straightened in her chair. For the first time, Penny could evaluate just how tall Nadine was; six foot two at least, and clad from head to toe in black, its denseness only relieved with base metal bangles and a collar that looked to be made of dull marcasite and leather and a good two inches in depth – perhaps made for a bull mastiff rather than a woman.

'No harm in that, my dears,' chirped up Sir

Reginald who Alistair had explained was a fellow
director and business associate in the wide and
varied group first founded by Alistair's father
before the Second World War. 'Perfection is to be
admired, my dears ... cosseted,' he added as his
broad hand circled Penny's back. She leaned forward away from the harp-shaped back of the chair.
His fingers spread downwards and slid over the
roundness of her buttocks. 'All perfection,' he
added with a low chuckle.

He smelt of expensive aftershave and his body
appeared well looked after beneath the expensive
smoothness of his black evening suit. Being of
mature age, and born with privilege and rank rather
than achieving it, he was the only one truly dressed
for dinner.

Alistair was not casually dressed, but not formally either. His shirt was made of grey silk that
matched his eyes. He wore a tie which must have
cost as much as some people would pay for a whole
outfit. He looked smooth, well-groomed and as
expensive as the neat gold-and-diamond cufflinks
that flashed at his wrists. Smooth, she thought, sure
of himself, yet strangely ill at ease; and the more he
looked at her, the more ill at ease he appeared to
become.

Not that he was the only one who studied her.
The expressions of everyone there were sympto-
matic of the fantasies each one was enjoying in their
minds.

All eyes relished the pertness of her nipples,
which were outlined like rare etchings through the
thin material of her dress.

Their eyes travelled, as though they were hands,

down to her waist and over the curve of her belly. Only Reggie could see any further. His eyes alighted on her lap. His breathing was quick and hot, his hand slightly sweaty upon her thigh, but pleasant.

With daring borrowed from the heaviness of the wine, she opened her legs slightly, and with one hand hitched her skirt a little higher. She heard Reggie suck in his breath as her own Black Forest came shyly into view; no more than a mass of darkness between the creamy flesh of her thighs.

Sidelong, she smiled at him, saw gratitude in his eyes and was rewarded for her efforts by his fingers edging stealthily over the soft satin of her inner thigh before tangling amongst her dusky hidden hair.

His lips were wet now, flecked with spittle at each corner. He licked them dry and smiled at her. Alistair talked to Auberon in the background, Nadine adding her more tart comments.

Yet somehow their talk was nothing more than a shadow, a mime they were going through as if to put her at her ease, to let her enjoy, to indulge and to arouse. There was more yet to come.

'I raise my glass to you,' he said with gentlemanly politeness, whilst the fingers of his right hand divided her feathered lips and touched lightly on her throbbing rosebud. 'I think you are a charming young woman, a great asset to this establishment and the association.'

'Association?' she queried. Her questioning tone merely disguised the moan that had escaped from her throat along with the word. She was wet, aroused and couldn't help her legs from opening wider. He took advantage of the opportunity. There was one finger now either side of her clitoris, each one folding her labia away from her innermost treasures.

He winked in a boyish way that complemented his handsome patrician features. A gold bracelet slid down his wrist as he raised his glass again.

'To you, young lady – and your association with everyone here.'

The two fingers slid towards her secret portal, dipped neatly in, retreated, then dipped again.

She was aware of her own breath quickening, her breasts rising and falling against her bodice, their curving edges peering out from the restriction of her dress like twin crescent moons. She was also aware that conversation had ceased, that she was the subject of silence and all-seeing eyes. But she didn't care. She was too far gone to care, too far along the road to a mind-shattering orgasm that she badly yearned for.

He drained his glass, she drained hers. She liked this man. Like Alistair, the power he possessed made her feel good, and secure. Now her glass was sadly empty. She lifted it and held it to the light so the wine turned pink against the lead crystal and the light from the chandeliers. As she twirled it, rainbow colours shot through each sharp cut prism of glass and threw its beam upon her face. Like people, she thought; or, at least, like the people here. White on the surface, but composed of many colours, with many facets.

'Is she very wet, Reggie darling?' Nadine asked suddenly.

Penny gasped, glanced swiftly at Alistair's sister,

then back, almost in a fit of pleading, to Reggie's face.

'Very wet, Nadine darling, very wet indeed. Just a little more effort, and this little pussy will come.'

Penny was speechless, as much from her mounting orgasm as from the sudden realisation that everyone there knew exactly what they were doing, and from the sound of it, *had* done all along.

'Then bring her off, darling. Right now!'

Like the prisms of light that had reflected so richly from the glass, the faces of those around Penny spun in a blur of colour as two fingers of Reggie's right hand pushed further into her. Never mind that everyone was watching. She was beyond caring. In an effort to capture the full impact of his fingers, she slid slightly forward on the chair so he could invade her more fully. All the while, his fingers dived in, his thumb dancing over her clitoris in short, sharp flicks. Now he used his other hand to hold back her fleshy lips and the sleek black hair of her pubes. And then it came, flooding over her in a torrent of electric release. Her hips lifted against his hands, and crying out, she threw her head back, closing her eyes, her orgasm diminishing with each murmur of breath.

Reggie removed his hands and washed them in the bowl of water at the side of his fork. The bowl was dark blue. A slice of lemon floated on the surface. It was a relaxed and effective action, emphasising cleanliness, opulence and sensuality at one and the same time.

Tossing her hair and still breathless, Penny eyed those around the table.

'Splendid, darling!' exclaimed Nadine, cheroot

gripped in her teeth and hands clapping. 'A splendid effort indeed. If you ride your horses like that, then you'll get no complaints from me.'

Auberon just smiled, and Reggie winked at her again, refilled his glass and raised it to her before sipping.

Alistair was staring at her, his mouth grim set and eyes glittering. She could see him swallowing consistently, and noticed that his lips were dry and that he seemed unable to say anything. Had he not seen enough? Or, perhaps, he had seen too much; perhaps she had blotted her copybook without meaning to.

At last, he cleared his throat. Then he spoke. 'Outstanding.'

Penny flashed her eyes as she savoured the word. That one word clarified exactly what he thought. Not the word itself: there was nothing much in that, it was ordinary, just a word. But she'd detected something else in the way he said it. Deep inside it had come into existence, yet had stuck in his throat, had grated its way to the surface so that when he *did* say it, its meaning was intensified. His voice had been as low as the depths from which it had come. She knew then that he wanted her, that in time her wager would be won.

Like liquid fire, she returned his stare with her own. When, she asked with her eyes, exactly when?

Alistair's gaze shifted, almost guiltily. From the centre of the table, he took hold of the half-empty wine bottle – one of three that sat on there – and poured into his own glass.

But other eyes watched. Other eyes surmised and made plans for these two people.

Nadine still held the key to her brother's torment. Thoughtfully, she played with the black cross that hung from her ear. It jingled playfully as she touched it. With each jingle, Penny noticed that Alistair's jaw clenched, and a nerve beneath his eye quivered.

Nadine saw her look but did not answer the question in her eyes. Nadine was taking pleasure from her brother's clenching jaw and the nerve that quivered just below his right eye. She knew what he was going through and understood how much the key, which hung behind the earring, meant to him. Only the shadow of a smile played around her mouth as she toyed with the earring and then touched the cold metal of the small key itself. Time and place was controlled by her. Nothing had changed, nothing would change. All in good time, her brother would have what he craved, and Penny would have more than she could ever have bargained for.

'More wine, Penny?'

Thoughts melted and scattered, Penny looked up into the soft, boyish face of Auberon Harding, another horse rider lucky enough to get a place under Beaumont's roof together with a wedge of his bank account.

'Yes please,' she replied. For some reason, she used her sexiest voice to answer. Perhaps it was because of the burning she felt deep inside; the need to have a male phallus inside her rather than just be played with, probed and brought off purely for the benefit of other people.

She smiled her thanks to Auberon Harding, the Honourable Auberon Harding to be exact, whose family were something in the meat trade and had been for generations. Perhaps they'd been high-street butchers who were suddenly landed with the privilege of supplying Queen Victoria with pork sausages. It didn't matter. Now, he was an Honourable, and he looked it. He had a look of class about him: thick lipped with a head-boy type of face and a hairstyle that sat firmly on the fence between fashion and conformity, yet flopped over his forehead. His clothes straddled the same fence. Not too formal, not too fashionable: white shirt; neat tie; neat jacket; neat, sharp-pleated trousers; polished black shoes. Everything about him was neat, correct, pleated and polished. Public school, she decided. She'd met others like him, men who found it impossible to shake off the residue of a rigid regime that had moulded them into a pre-set shape. It was as if they'd originally been made of jelly and now were cast in bronze.

He looked nice enough, but, although he surveyed her dark hair, her open expression and her gaping neckline, she was surprised and a mite disappointed when his eyes did not linger.

Fragments of conversation filtered into Penny's mind as she drank more wine, which was smooth on her tongue and mellow in her head. On top of that, the newness of everything, the excitement of it all and the experience of her dining-table orgasm had lightened her mind even more. Eager to learn and perhaps experience more, she continued to survey those at the table, her dark lashes sweeping her cheeks as her eyes flickered from one guest to another along with the conversation.

Sir Reginald fondled her knee each time he spoke

to her. There was something strangely protective about his fondling, as though he were trying to put her at ease and to make her feel at home. She let him, and tried her best to let Alistair know that she was letting him. After all, there was still the wager to consider, though gradually she was becoming fascinated with this close group of people who had accepted her so easily and so completely.

For the moment, her massage with the blond angel was forgotten, though if nothing further came off tonight, she would need him again, if only to ease her aching libido with his flexible fingers, though she would of course prefer his rampant penis.

But Gregory was not here. Alistair was. She caught him looking at her once or twice. It was a guilty look, as though he was a small boy and had been caught stealing from a sweet shop. So far, she thought to herself, Alistair had disappointed her.

Adopting an air of indifference to hide that disappointment, she let her eyes study the other diners whilst her mind weighed up each one.

Sir Reggie was sweet, debonair and highly attractive. She imagined that having sex with him would be a very professional experience. During his life, he would have known many women, would have indulged most readily in every conceivable practice and with every conceivable age, colour and creed of woman. Sir Reggie had been in the army. Sir Reggie had travelled.

Auberon seemed the height of politeness, the warmth between them like one old schoolmate to another whenever he included her in his conversation. There was no strange guilt in his look like there was with Alistair. His colouring and flickering eyelids came more from shyness than guilt. Of course, she still couldn't quite work out what Alistair had to be guilty about.

Nadine was the most intense watcher. Each time Penny chanced to look in her direction, Nadine was staring back at her over the top of her wineglass, and although Alistair dominated the conversation with his talk of mergers, expansion and then the world of equestrianism, she had a distinct impression his sister might be more powerful than him.

Watching and wondering about her fellow diners ignited new excitement in Penny's loins. The actions and the scenes she envisaged each of these people in were only in her mind at present, yet she knew that what could be fantasised could also be turned into fact.

As she sipped her wine, she imagined what each man's body would feel like against hers, what each sex would feel like in her as each mouth nibbled and sucked at her willing breasts.

Her eyes darted to each in turn and her mind visualised virulently before settling on Alistair. There was something about him that was simultaneously alluring and secretive. She was drawn to him, and everything Ariadne had said only added to her curiosity. Like getting to grips with a new horse, he was a challenge, a creature to be broken and ridden. Vaguely, she knew in her mind that whatever it took, she would have him.

Ariadne had told her he was a voyeur, a spectator. Then, she decided, she would give him plenty to look at. Each and every sexual encounter she had would be within his sight so he would have to take part and would be unable to resist the depths to which debauchery and her own sexuality could plumb. She drained her glass. With a smile, Auberon refilled it.

Food, wine and sparkling conversation were all in plentiful supply. As the wine poured down her throat, she began to wonder who was on offer this evening, who was there for the asking and where Alistair would be when she indulged her desire.

'Lovely meal, my dear, don't you think?' The plump-fingered hand of the errant knight squeezed her thigh, his fingers lightly touching the valley at the top of her legs.

She smiled at him, then over at Alistair. He glanced at her, almost as if he knew what was happening.

Turning to Sir Reginald, and looking into his face as though he were the lover she had always been waiting for, she opened her legs a little wider. She saw his lips get wetter, the bottom one sagging. Purposefully, she snapped her legs shut. Sir Reggie's hand retreated and his eyes flickered. He looked hurt for a moment, but only for a moment. His smile returned and he turned his face and his conversation to Alistair.

A gentle touch on her elbow made her transfer her attention to Auberon. There was a fairy lightness in his fingers, a playfulness that betrayed the strength needed for the sport he so lovingly pursued. Reins were hard to hold on a plunging, rearing animal that weighed something near half a ton, and didn't she know it?

'It's nice to have you here. It really is so terribly

nice.' She smiled at him and to herself. He even sounded like a head boy – one left over from some obscure and ancient public school.

And yet there was sincerity in his eyes and on his lips. She was aware of sudden silence. Conversation, which up until now had flowed almost unabated except when Penny had attracted their attention, had now ceased. Suddenly, she felt as though she were the centre of attention.

Briefly, she glanced towards Alistair. His eyes met hers before he leaned across the table and spoke to Sir Reginald. She couldn't grasp what was said. She looked from the older man to the younger, then was aware of the eyes of Alistair's sister, Nadine. They were like pale grey pools amid the heavy black make-up. And suddenly, along with everyone else, there was lust in her eyes.

Holding Nadine's gaze and tensing her back, Penny clenched her buttocks in an effort to control the familiar ache surging between her thighs. There were opportunities here, she told herself, and though her vision was blurred and her head was light, she had no intention of missing them.

'Do you think you will like it here?' Auberon asked her.

Everyone seemed to be holding their breath for her answer. All, she guessed, needed to know how her earlier sojourn with Sir Reggie had affected her opinion.

'It's nice to be here. It really is,' she said brightly. 'Am I right in thinking you've got the room below me?' She placed her hand on his thigh, felt the iron-hard muscles tense beneath her touch.

Around the table, there was a sudden exhalation

of breath, as though there had been a doubt, which was now discarded.

But Penny was only half-aware now of what was happening around her. She made no secret of what she was doing at the table, her smile wide, whilst her fingers flicked gently but determinedly at the awakening flesh just behind Auberon's zip-fastener. Here was a flower just waiting to be plucked, and she had just the vase to put it in, she thought cheerily.

He flushed as he nodded, and his eyes flitted briefly around the table. Other mouths smiled, other eyes sparkled as though they too were experiencing what he was experiencing. Nervously, his tongue licked at his lips. As his leg moved, his shaft jumped against his trousers.

And yet, there was a vulnerability about him, an innocence that seemed strangely irreconcilable with the determined sportsman she knew him to be. She retrieved her hand and smiled.

I wonder, she thought to herself, head supported on cupped hand whilst her other hand twirled the dark liquid in her glass, whether he's a bit of a cane man – even a bit gay.

'Time for bed.' Alistair got to his feet. As if it were a prescribed signal, everyone else got to theirs.

Sir Reginald coughed and yawned in disjointed unison, and Penny smiled into her wine as the shiny seat of his well-polished dinner trousers came into view.

Nadine rose in chilly black splendour like a winter's night, head and shoulders above everyone present.

She was silent, though her eyes glittered and

flitted briefly from one face to another before ending up on Penny. There was no disguising the self-congratulation in her look. As though she's looking through my clothes rather than at them, thought Penny. It was as if, she reflected, weakly grasping the thought as it circled in her mind, that Nadine knew exactly what was underneath. It was then she remembered her suspicions about the mirror and also about Alistair being a man who watched, not did. There were no guesses as to who he'd be watching tonight.

'I'll be taking a stroll, if anyone wants to join me.' Sir Reginald's now bloodshot eyes searched for an offer.

No one did join him.

All the same, Penny was aware of knowing glances passing from one to the other. A curling feeling rose and fell in her stomach. Somehow she knew that no matter where she went to bed that night or what she did, someone would be watching.

Odalisque

Fleur Reynolds

Odalisque was Fleur Reynolds' first Black Lace book. Set against a backdrop of sophisticated elegance, the story unravels the intrigues, bitter rivalries and sordid secrets of one wealthy family. Auralie and Jeanine are cousins locked into a sexual feud. This is like *Dallas* with extra deparavity!

Fleur went on to write three other books for Black Lace. They are: *Handmaiden of Palmyra* (set in 3rd-century Syria), *The House in New Orleans* (contemporary USA) and *Conquered* (set in 16th-century Peru).

Odalisque

~∞~

*A*uralie put three bottles of Krug into the office refrigerator. It was her favourite champagne and she knew today she would have something to celebrate. Having done that, she glanced at the clock, saw the time and slipped out of the jeans, sweater, bra and panties she wore in the workroom and took a quick shower. She had had the bathroom put in so that she could transform herself at a moment's notice.

Hanging in the closet was her new, fabulously expensive white cashmere suit. She had bought it especially for the occasion. Today was the day she and Olga would make their presentation to De Bouys Airlines. Today would be the day she would get the contract. She couldn't fail. Her designs were the best, the very best she had ever done. They were bright and innovative and besides, she held the ace: she was Sir Henry's daughter-in-law. The telephone rang. She let it ring. Moments later there was a knock on the door.

'Mrs de Bouys. Mrs de Bouys.' It was her secretary's voice. She sounded extremely agitated.

'Yes?' queried Auralie.

'Madame Olga is on the phone. She says it is very important.'

Auralie leisurely picked up her extension.

'Auralie, today is postponed,' said Olga, mysteriously but with a hint of mischief in her voice.

'What!' exclaimed Auralie.

'I've just heard from Sir Henry's secretary. Apparently he's stopped off in Rome. Some urgent business.'

'But . . .' said Auralie.

'The girl said he'll be ringing her later. She expects him in England tonight so there's a possibility of tonight or tomorrow morning. We just have to wait.'

'That's terrible news,' said Auralie.

'Not really, *chérie*,' purred Olga. 'I'll pick you up in ten minutes and we can go to the apartment. I've given Sir Henry's secretary the number. She can ring us there.'

Auralie immediately dispensed with her panties, brassiere and the white cashmere suit. She took down another set of clothes and over her bare, neat, pert, upright breasts she put on and buttoned up a heavy, translucent slub silk blouse. She stepped into a black leather skirt which hugged her hips then fell in graceful bias cut folds over her slim, suntanned thighs. She sat down to apply some extra lipstick, enjoying the feel of the leather against her bare bottom. She put on her highest high-heels. Auralie possessed neatly pinched-in ankles and the height of her shoes accentuated their shape. She

238

knew what Olga wanted. She knew what Olga liked. She also knew what *she* liked and wanted. Auralie wondered if Olga had brought her entire entourage with her, or only her chauffeur. If it was only the chauffeur she wondered if it was the same one as last time.

Picking up her handbag and notebook, saying goodbye to her secretary with a reminder to put on the burglar alarm, Auralie stepped out into the smart Mayfair street as Olga's blacked-out white limousine drew alongside the kerb.

Auralie noticed the chauffeur was new, young and very beautiful. He was also very black. He held the door open for her. She smiled, inwardly. Wantonly. A certain familiar feeling, an anticipation, a sudden welcome juiciness flowed through her loins. She could feel a tingling gripping her belly, finding its release in the delicious wetness that began to flow as her sex unfurled.

Olga, attractive and patrician, was perfectly coiffured and made-up. With her long, high, almost beak-like nose, and eyes that slanted as if way back in her ancestry there was Mongolian blood, there was something magnificently savage about her. She held her straight mouth with a disdainful air. Tall, in her late thirties and elegantly swathed in flowing chiffon, Olga lounged back with the ease and haughtiness of the very rich and waited for Auralie to get into the car. Olga stretched out a bejewelled hand. The two women smiled at each other, a secret conspiratorial smile. The chauffeur closed the door. Before she could sit down Olga ran her hand up and over Auralie's thighs. She squeezed her bare buttocks.

'Good girl,' she said. 'Immediately accessible. I hope you are wet, *chérie*.'

Insolently, with no foreplay, Olga pitched her long and elegant forefinger into Auralie's moist, lascivious pussy. Auralie gasped audibly with the sudden rush of pleasure. Moving that finger backwards and forwards Olga quickly found the entrance to Auralie's anus and penetrated that with her ring finger. Excited and willingly impaled by her lover's fingers, Auralie squirmed. Olga gripped the whole of Auralie's black mound, forced her back against the leather seat and kissed her mouth. With every orifice plundered Auralie let out squeals of bliss. This was what she liked, what she had been waiting for. Olga's touch. Olga, who knew exactly what to do and how to do it. Olga, who could make her feel first sexy, then erotic and sensual, and finally completely abandoned.

'Miss me?' Olga asked.

Auralie turned slightly and smiled. Olga's fingers were making her wetter with every second. Auralie pushed back her shoulders so that Olga could see her erect nipples straining through the fabric of her blouse.

'Yes,' replied Auralie.

'Then show it,' said Olga.

Auralie knelt between Olga's legs, parted her chiffon skirt, revealing lacy stocking tops then Olga's total nakedness to the waist. Olga put her own hands between her legs and displayed herself, allowing Auralie to see how much she desired her. She moved her hips from side to side. Auralie rubbed a finger along Olga's swollen sex lips, softly touching the stiffening bud at the top. Olga tensed her muscles, silently asking for increased pressure on her clitoris. Auralie obeyed, and Olga gave a tiny gasp of delight and began kneading her own breasts. Auralie, looking at Olga lying lewdly on the leather seat, her legs apart, her hips raised, her sex being played with, thought she bore a greater resemblance to an expensive strumpet than the boss of a multi-million dollar industry. Auralie began to ease her fingers inwards, feeling the delight of the soft ridges, the tender juiciness of Olga's beautifully made mound.

Olga undid the buttons of Auralie's blouse. Auralie pushed her flat little tongue through her neat pearly white teeth and wiggled it suggestively. Olga narrowed her eyes and smiled like a cat. The two women stared at one another, playing a familiar game of excitation. Olga reached out a hand and grabbed at one of Auralie's hard nipples. Auralie bent her head. Olga raised her hips but Auralie did not do as she was expecting. She didn't put her tongue to Olga's ripened opening; instead she took her legs and, with a sudden harshness, spread them further apart and stroked and kneaded the sensual flesh at the top of Olga's thighs.

Olga, panting, raised her hips higher, offering herself to Auralie who finally buried her tongue in Olga's sweet perfumed, rosy flesh. She licked her. She teased her. Olga stroked herself, letting Auralie see how wet and open she was, how much she desired the other woman. She began sliding her hips from side to side and rubbing her fingers along her swollen inner fleshy walls, opening up her vulva. Auralie moved her tongue along Olga's swollen edges, her nose devouring her smell. Then she bit gently on the engorged clitoris. Olga lay back, her hands playing with Auralie's breasts, and moaned with abandonment. Auralie put her fingers beside her tongue at Olga's private opening and waited. She felt Olga's muscles quicken with anticipation. She felt her quiver and tremble. Auralie quickly, sharply and suddenly penetrated Olga's sex with the forefinger of her right hand, her other forefinger invaded her anus. To the roar of the traffic, to the sound of engines and car horns, Auralie continued to suck on Olga's clitoris while fingering both her orifices. Then they rolled on to the floor of the car and began touching each other, feeling each other, sucking each other, wallowing in each other's soft, creamy sensitive, wet, pliable sex. They played until the car came to a halt.

'Madam, we are here,' came the chauffeur's voice through the intercom.

'Two moments,' replied Olga, giving them time to adjust their clothing before alighting at Olga's short-rent apartment.

Olga did not keep a London home. When she was in England she usually stayed at Petrov's mansion in the country, but if spending more than two days in town she took short-let accommodation. The owner of her present apartment was a long-time friend. He let it to Olga, at a price, on a fairly regular basis. It suited her needs more than a protracted stay at a hotel where all her comings and goings could be watched and spied upon.

'Leave nothing in the car,' Olga told the chauffeur imperiously before she and Auralie swept into the lobby of one of Kensington's prime mansion blocks and entered a waiting elevator.

'How new is he?' Auralie asked, referring to the chauffeur.

'Kensit? Very,' said Olga.

'Has he been . . .?'

'No, *chérie*. Not yet,' said Olga wickedly as the elevator reached their floor. Nicole, the maid, opened the door before Olga rang the bell. She must have known, must have watched our arrival, thought Auralie, but then she had been with Olga for a couple of years. Olga would have given her a time. Nicole would have known exactly when to open the door.

The pretty maid in her little outfit, a black frock with frilly white apron and a little white lace cap, curtsied. Her frock was brought in tightly at the waist with a wide elastic waspie belt. She was wearing high-heeled, lace-up shoes that made her arse jut out curvaceously, emphasising her very full breasts.

'There is someone waiting for you, madam,' Nicole said as the two women entered the terracotta coloured hall, their footsteps echoing on the parquet floor. Olga and Auralie exchanged glances. Auralie deliberately walked behind the maid looking at her gait, her shape and her frock. She could see through the split from waist to hem loose-fitting, pink satin knickers. Auralie had a strong desire to run her hands up the maid's legs under the pink satin and feel the girl's bottom.

Olga suddenly rounded on her maid and checked that every button on her uniform was securely fastened. 'And may they stay that way, Nicole,' she added, menacingly.

'Yes, madam,' said the girl, as Olga's hand

splayed and each finger pressed softly over the maid's breasts. Nicole took in a short sharp breath of pleasure and anticipation, then swallowing over a lump in her throat she glanced shyly away and blushed deeply.

'But why is she wearing knickers?' asked Auralie maliciously.

'You're wearing knickers, Nicole!' exclaimed Olga.

'Sorry, madam,' said the maid, contritely.

'Sorry is not good enough. Let me see. Bend over and show me this instant,' ordered Olga.

Nicole bent over obediently. Her frock parted revealing the pink satin drawers.

'You know that is against the rules,' said Olga, 'and you'll have to be punished. Auralie, pull down her drawers.'

Savagely, and with some satisfaction, Auralie pulled the girl's panties down to her ankles, leaving her beautifully rounded bare bottom exposed. At that moment the new chauffeur entered the apartment. He stopped in amazement, then quickly tried to cover the sudden bulge in his trousers with the bags he was carrying. He was not quite quick enough. Both Olga and Auralie had already noticed his reaction.

'Take those bags through to the kitchen,' commanded Olga, pointing along the corridor. The chauffeur did as he was told and Olga's attention returned to Nicole.

'A bare bottom, Nicole,' said Olga, giving the maid a swinging swipe as if to reinforce her statement. The girl's cheeks immediately flushed pink. 'A bare bottom at all times.'

'Yes, madam,' said the maid, not moving from her position.

'Miss Auralie will punish you in a moment. First I want a cocktail. A Bellini. What'll you have, *chérie*?'

'The same,' Auralie replied, licking her lips in anticipation, but not for the cocktail. She desperately wanted to touch the maid's body, her breasts, the top of her thighs, between her thighs, and her bare bottom. She knew she would have her pleasure very soon.

'Go,' said Olga.

'But, madam,' said Nicole. 'You're forgetting that there is someone waiting to see you. Her name is Margaret. She's come from Monsieur Petrov. I've put her in the study.'

'Margaret? From Petrov?' queried Auralie. 'What's she like, Nicole?'

'Not very tall,' replied the maid, 'plump, quite pretty.'

A smile of recognition crossed Auralie's lips.

'You know her?' Olga asked Auralie, giving the maid a dismissive wave.

'Yes,' said Auralie.

'You have had her?' asked Olga.

'Oh, yes,' said Auralie, smiling, remembering with salacious pleasure a recent afternoon at her home.

'And . . .?' said Olga.

'She has definite potential,' replied Auralie.

Olga and Auralie walked into the drawing-room. It was magnificently furnished with exceptionally high windows leading on to a balcony overlooking the park. Auralie sat on a sage green, velvet covered chaise-longue. Olga stood against the black marble fireplace, absentmindedly playing with an arrangement of brightly coloured exotic flowers and bamboo canes.

'Your designs are beautiful,' said Olga, approvingly. '*Très chic, chérie, très chic*. I am sure we will get the contract. The designs, the colours, the fabric, everything. We will win. It is impossible for us to fail. And we mustn't fail, *chérie*. Because, well you know the consequences! The de Bouys contract has to fill the gap left by Krakos. Why did he have to die? The fool! Even more of a fool to leave everything to his spoilt brat daughter. What a thing she did to sell her father's lifetime's work. Sell all those liners. You know not one did she keep. Not one. Not one for us to redecorate, redesign, refurbish. So we have to have Sir Henry's contract. Without it Petolg Holdings, the factory, the company, everything is, how you say in English? A dead duck. *Finito*. Finished.'

'I know,' said Auralie.

'That girl is taking a long time to make two cocktails!' said Olga.

'Isn't she!' replied Auralie, enigmatically.

'So, *chérie*. Tell me, how is your little cousin?' asked Olga.

'Fine,' said Auralie. She didn't want to think or talk about Jeanine.

'And her hotel; is that fine too?'

'I believe so,' said Auralie. She had never let Olga know the depth of her hatred for Jeanine. Nobody had any idea that she had sent two of her old lovers to be chambermaids at Jeanine's. And nobody had any idea what she had told them to do whilst they were there. 'Yes, Olga, everything with Jeanine is absolutely fine.' Auralie felt the need to reassure her.

'Petrov tells me she hasn't been to see him recently. Do you know why?'

'No.'

'Ah well, business I suppose. Perhaps you and I should pay her a visit ...' Olga stopped abruptly and rang the bell pull. A moment later the maid appeared bringing in their cocktails. 'What have you been doing, Nicole?'

'Making the cocktails, madam.'

'Making the cocks more like it,' said Olga.

'Oh no, madam. No,' said the maid, trembling. With lowered eyes she placed the two glasses on the table.

'Nicole, I asked you a question. What have you been doing?'

'Nothing madam. Nothing.'

'You expect me to believe that? Where is my new chauffeur?'

'He's in the bathroom, madam.'

'In the bathroom! And what's he doing in the bathroom?'

'I don't know, madam.'

'You don't know! Come here.'

Shaking slightly, Nicole stood in front of Olga.

'You don't know! I think you are lying, Nicole. I think he's in the bathroom waiting to screw you.'

'No, madam, no.'

'Nicole, I think you have been showing my new chauffeur your nice fat arse. I think ...' Olga took a bamboo cane from the vase beside her and staring into Nicole's big blue eyes began to lift the hem of

247

the maid's frock with the stick. 'I think you have been letting him lift the hem of your skirt.'

'No, madam, oh no,' replied Nicole earnestly, wondering what else her mistress was going to do with the cane.

'Oh yes, I think you have been letting him lift your skirt, and ...' said Olga. 'I think you have been letting him play with your pussy.' Very slowly and with great assuredness Olga let the cane trail along her maid's sex-lips, teasing, pressing on, but never entering the girl's willing wetness.

'No, madam, no. I wouldn't,' said Nicole, breathless and squirming, making tiny little rolling movements wih her hips. She was trying to make Olga let the hard pencil-thin cane accidentally glide into her silken warm opening.

'And I think you let him undo the buttons and let him feel your tits.'

'No, madam, no.'

Olga ran a finger down the front of the girl's frock, counting as she went. She got to button number three and found it gaping open.

'No?'

'No, madam,' the maid whispered tremulously.

Olga continued counting and checking, finding numbers four and five undone as well.

'Then what's this?' said Olga angrily.

'Oh no ... no ...' the maid's hands flew to her breasts in a vain attempt to hide the offending opening in her clothing.

'One, Nicole. One I could have forgiven, but three!'

Almost before the maid realised, Olga thrust Nicole's hands away and forced her own hands

248

inside the girl's frock. She squeezed Nicole's stiff excited nipples. 'Auralie, see, there is a gap here big enough for me to put my hands inside. And if I can do it, he can too. Nicole, aren't you ashamed of yourself?'

Enjoying the erotic sureness of her mistress's touch, Nicole lowered her head as if admitting her disgraceful behaviour. Olga tweaked the girl's nipples again. Auralie sipped her Bellini. Every minute that went by, every minute that Olga chastised her maid, humiliated her, touched and felt and played with her private places made Auralie more and more horny. She was still waiting to caress the girl's fat bottom. She wanted to feel its lusciousness quivering beneath her touch. And she wanted to smack it. Slap it. She also wanted to feel between the girl's legs. Touch the open wet juiciness at the top of her thighs.

'Auralie,' said Olga, grabbing the maid's wrists and pinioning her arms behind her back, 'did I or did I not check that all her buttons were done up when we arrived?'

'You did,' said Auralie.

'And she wants us to believe that she hasn't let the chauffeur touch her. *Chérie*, lift her skirt. Feel her. Feel her pussy. I think you'll find it's very wet.'

Whilst Olga kept the maid's hands locked behind her back Auralie snaked her way across the room then lifted the maid's frock. Nicole let out little gasps of pleasure as Auralie's fingers slid all too easily into her extremely moist sex.

'Very wet indeed,' Auralie pronounced, shoving her fingers up and down inside the maid's sex, making Nicole dance, making her squirm.

249

'*Chérie*,' said Olga, 'would you say that whilst we were sitting here, thirsty, waiting for our drink, this slut was being felt and screwed by my new chauffeur?'

'I would say there was every chance of that,' replied Auralie, knowing how well the maid's soft flesh was responding to her moving fingers.

'No, madam, I didn't,' protested the maid.

'You know my rules,' said Olga. 'You do not touch a man, or allow him to touch you unless we give you permission.'

'But I didn't, madam, I didn't.'

'We think you did, and you know what happens when you break the rules don't you, Nicole?'

'Yes, madam.'

Olga undid the remaining buttons on the top half of Nicole's frock, letting her full breasts spill out. Olga brought her mouth down, allowing her tongue to flick across the maid's soft brown nipples.

'You have to be punished,' said Olga sweetly. 'Auralie, tuck the hem of her skirt into her belt.'

Reluctantly Auralie withdrew her fingers from the girl's sex and did as she was told. Olga reached into the flower arrangement and picked out another bamboo cane. This one was extra thin and extra long.

'Your pleasure, *chérie*,' said Olga, testing the cane for spring then handing it to Auralie, who smiled wickedly, licentiously.

'Bend over, Nicole,' commanded Olga.

'No, madam, I didn't. I didn't touch him. Please, no, don't cane me, please.'

'Bend and take your punishment!' said Olga, ignoring the girl's pleas and pointing to the raised end of the chaise-longue. Nicole bent over. Auralie placed a cushion between the arm of the chaise-longue and Nicole's belly, raising the girl's bottom higher. Smiling, Auralie now had the maid exactly how she wanted her. She massaged the maid's rounded, expectant bottom. Then, pulling the girl's arms out ahead of her, made sure her voluptuous breasts were hanging free. Auralie thought Nicole was ready for her punishment, but Nicole knew what really aroused her mistress. She gave a tiny sigh then let her fat white buttocks go loose and floppy. Later she would have her reward. She would be allowed to crawl between her mistress's legs and suck her pussy. And she knew the more Olga enjoyed the spectacle of her being caned, the longer her fat little tongue would be able to slurp at her mistress's juices. Meanwhile she was longing to feel the harsh sharp bliss of that strip of thin springy bamboo scorching and marking her white buttocks.

Olga smiled her cat-like smile as the girl bent over; so wet, so willing, and waiting for the stripe to sear down across her bare bottom. Auralie trailed the thin cane up between the maid's legs. Then, with tiny circular movements, poked first at her arse then at her soft open sex. The maid quivered with excitement as the thin hardness of the cane touched her hidden rosy, creamy-wet flesh.

'Six, Auralie,' said Olga sternly.

Nicole caught and held her breath as Auralie brought the cane swishing down over Nicole's round buttocks. Between each stripe Auralie rammed her fingers into the girl's sex. The exquisite mixture of pain and pleasure almost brought Nicole to the point of orgasm. She tried to contain herself, not wanting Auralie to see how much she was enjoying her punishment. Each time the cane came down Nicole cried out, begging Auralie to stop, but to no avail. Auralie knew exactly what she was doing. She loved the feeling of control and the sight of the deep red weals on Nicole's tender fleshy bottom. After the sixth stripe Auralie threw away the cane and sat on an easy chair. Wetter than before, more excited than before, Auralie lifted the black leather of her own skirt and began to rub her fingers along her own sex. Olga glanced at her enjoying herself. She knew Auralie's fingers had found their fountain of pleasure. Olga smiled as Auralie sighed deeply with satisfaction. Then, Olga inspected the criss-cross of red weals on Nicole's bottom. She gently kissed and caressed the marks left by the cane.

'Now, what do you say, Nicole?' said Olga walking away and sitting on a chair in the far corner of the room.

'Thank you, madam, thank you.'

'And how are you going to show your thanks, your true thanks?'

Auralie, who now had her own legs wide apart, her thumb on her clitoris and two fingers inside herself watched lecherously as the maid crawled to where Olga was sitting.

Nicole knelt between Olga's outstretched legs. She removed Olga's shoes, then her stockings, and as she did so she stroked the soft erogenous zone of Olga's inner thighs. Nicole bent her head and, parting Olga's chiffon skirt, and with due reverence, sank her fat little tongue into her mistress's pussy.

'Thank you, madam,' said Nicole, remaining on her knees and greedily licking and slurping at her employer's sex.

Olga lay back, her arms over the side of the chair and her legs spread wide apart, doing nothing except lapping up the feeling of total abandonment and the precise touch of her maid's expert little tongue. From time to time she glanced at Auralie who was still playing with herself, sighing and gently enjoying her clitoris, but not allowing herself to come.

'You may get up, Nicole,' said Olga after a while, 'but your dress stays where it is. We want to be able to see those delightful buttocks. You won't break the rules again, will you?'

'No, madam.'

'Now, you wanted to screw my chauffeur?'

'No, madam.'

'But isn't he beautiful? Isn't he desirable?'

'Yes, madam. But I don't want to screw him, madam.'

'Then you will have to do something you don't want to do.'

'No madam, please. No.'

The maid fell down to the ground and crawled towards Olga again. Olga watched her impassively.

'Nicole, do you want to remain my maid?'

'Yes, madam.'

'Well, then you understand what that means, don't you? You do everything for my pleasure,' said Olga, bending the girl over her knees and making gentle soft affectionate circular movements over her marked bare bottom with both her hands. 'It is my pleasure to watch you being screwed. I want to see you sitting on him. I want to see his big black prick going up inside you, making you shudder. And I hope it is a big black prick,' mused Olga, almost absentmindedly.

'It is, madam, it is.' The words were out before Nicole realised what she had said.

'What!' Olga brought one hand down on the girl's backside with a loud resonant slap at the same time as the fingers of her other hand expertly jabbed into her sex and anus, impaling her wickedly and deliciously.

'You lied to me. I knew you'd been playing with him,' said Olga. 'I knew it. So, where is he now?'

Nicole stayed silent. Olga teased her maid's clitoris. Nicole was making exquisite little movements of enjoyment with her hips.

'Come on, tell me.' Olga jabbed her fingers viciously into her maid's lewd pussy.

'I left him in the bathroom, naked,' Nicole finally admitted.

'Completely naked?' said Auralie, coming over and stroking Olga's breasts whilst Olga continued to play with the maid. 'Nothing on?'

'Nothing except a blindfold,' replied Nicole.

'A blindfold?' asked Auralie.

'Yes.'

'You are a wicked girl,' said Olga. 'A very wicked girl to tell me such lies.'

'I wanted to watch him wanking.'

'Wanking! Wanking!'

'Playing with himself.'

'You deserve a good whipping,' said Olga, and

she felt the girl's muscles twitch in anticipation. 'But now you are going to screw my chauffeur. You are going to screw Kensit.'

Olga pushed the girl off her lap. Auralie pulled her up and grabbed her hand.

'Now do it, and don't you dare disobey me,' said Olga, taking an elbow-length pair of black leather gloves from her handbag and putting them on. Then she followed Auralie as she dragged the reluctant maid out of the room.

They found Kensit in the bathroom, sitting on the ebony wood lavatory seat facing the door. He looked superb, and Auralie's eyes narrowed as she smiled greedily. In the 1930s bathroom, which still had the original black and white tiles and white porcelain furniture, his black body glistened harmoniously. With her designer's eye Auralie decided he looked perfect. With her sexual eyes she knew he was breathtaking. He was naked except for a bandana covering his eyes. Auralie took a deep breath. He was sinuously beautiful and his muscles rippled as he sat playing with his very erect penis. Auralie wanted him. She wanted to feel his shaft inside her. It was hard and upright, a penis in full glory. It was neither too big nor too small. It was, thought Auralie, the perfect shape and size. She stuck out her tongue and wiggled it in lustful approval. Kensit heard the movement at the door.

'Is that you, Nicole?'

Olga curtly shoved her maid into the room, indicating she straddle the naked Kensit. Nicole gave her employer a 'do I really have to' look and then obeyed her mistress.

'Yes, it's me,' whispered Nicole into Kensit's ear.

'You were a long time,' he said, with one hand stroking his cock and the other cupping his balls.

'Yes, there were things I had to do for them,' Nicole replied enigmatically.

Kensit reached up and felt for Nicole's pendulous breasts. Nicole closed Kensit's legs and stood facing him. She turned her head to look at Olga, who gave a nod of encouragement.

Holding on to Kensit's shoulders Nicole hovered over his stiff prick, then very slowly let him feel the merest whisper of her wet sex on his swollen tip. Kensit gasped. He wanted to shove it straight up and ride her, but Nicole had other ideas. Nibbling at his ear, she pulled up and away from him.

'No, not yet,' she whispered, hovering again. Nicole was determined to take a number of pleasures instantaneously. She was going to make her mistress and Auralie wait for as long as possible before they enjoyed the sight of his black prick entering her juicy wet sex. She knew the thrill they would get from watching his cock slide into her, watching that hard knob push her open, then its black shaft inch its way upwards further and further into her squashy, pink, swollen, lustful flesh. She also knew what those two bitches would be doing to each other the moment she had Kensit's cock rammed hard inside her. They would start playing with each other's pussy and tits. Well, they could wait. This time she was in control. And besides, she wanted to feel the full impact of Kensit's pleasure, taking her, stretching her, screwing her. Screwing her fast and furiously, his anticipation finally realised.

Pressing her hands down on his shoulders so that

they were taking her full weight, Nicole very gradually let his prick feel its way inside her hungry sex. Kensit gasped and moulded her breasts with his hands. Then just when he had got used to her soft luscious gliding rhythm, suddenly, and with one quick movement, she thrust down, taking his thick engorged prick up to the hilt. She devoured him; she took every inch of him until there was no gap between his belly and her belly, no gap between his body and her body. With one fast jerk she had taken him completely. She rode him like a horse.

He was still unaware of Olga's and Auralie's presence. They watched lasciviously from the doorway as Nicole's reddened bottom rose and fell. They were enjoying the vicarious pleasure of seeing Kensit's proud member penetrate Nicole's lush wet opening. The beauty of Kensit's erect black penis sliding deeper and deeper into the maid's debauched sex was not lost upon them. With her hands encased in the fine black leather gloves Olga began to undo the buttons on Auralie's silk blouse. Lifting Olga's chiffon skirt, Auralie lent back against the doorpost and gently rubbed Olga's clitoris as Olga massaged Auralie's breasts. Teetering on her high-heels Auralie braced herself as Olga's hands travelled over her body. She tensed her buttock muscles as she felt the gloved hand slowly slide up her legs. Auralie swayed from side to side as the seams of the gloves touched the delicate malleable flesh beyond her pubis. Aware of the need for silence, Auralie held back the gasp of delight as Olga rammed her leather-covered fingers harshly inside her. The two women, stimulating each other, continued to watch Kensit's member thrusting harder and harder into the maid. They watched with pure pleasure as they saw him stretching her sex and his large black hands holding her fat white bottom whenever Nicole took an upward motion, forcing it back down again. Auralie stroked Olga's inner thighs as Olga's gloved hand penetrated deeper and deeper, imprisoning her on the moving shaft of black leather. Kensit's prick was moving faster and faster too. Up and down. Fast and furious. Auralie began to want the cock. Want Kensit's cock inside her. She wanted to take that beautiful prick into her and enclose her flesh around its erect hardness. Kensit was almost on the point of orgasm when Nicole, turning and seeing Auralie's wanton expression, suddenly stopped moving.

'No,' cried Kensit.

'One moment,' Nicole whispered. And before the man could realise what was happening, Nicole had withdrawn and Auralie had taken her place. Olga and Nicole left the room. Auralie sat on Kensit's penis, used her muscles to squeeze him back to extra hard, then removed his blindfold.

'Jeez!' he exclaimed, 'I thought you were the maid. She left me here, said she was coming back to screw me. Told me to play with myself and said to put the blindfold on, it's more sexy.'

'So it is,' said Auralie, starting to ride the slightly bemused young man. 'You like to screw?'

'Sure,' said Kensit.

'Then you're in luck,' she said, confusing Kensit even more by removing herself from his hard member.

'But . . .'

'No buts. Follow me,' said Auralie, and led the naked man through to the study across the hall.

Auralie opened the study door. There was Margaret, the girl sent from Petrov, dressed in a black habit, her face hidden by the hood. She was kneeling in supplication on the floor.

'This girl,' said Auralie to Kensit, pointing to the figure whose clothed bottom was raised up and facing them, 'has secret desires. Unbecoming desires. She has told her Confessor she has been dreaming about sex. Sex with men, sex with women, sex with strangers. Wicked dreams, Kensit, wouldn't you agree? Do you know why she's kneeling like that? I will tell you. She wants to be screwed. She's waiting for it. And we would like you to take her.'

Auralie stood astride the girl, facing Kensit and gazing lasciviously at his prick. Keeping her eyes on the man, Auralie rolled back the girl's black habit, revealing her plump, white bare legs with chains attached to her ankles, which were attached to a large ring on the wall. Long, navy blue serge drawers covered her raised bottom.

'Pull down her drawers,' ordered Auralie.

Kensit's cock quivered. He bent over and pulled her knickers down to her knees. Auralie, excited by Kensit's hard prick, leant forward and took it in her mouth. Sensual, incredible and very erotic thoughts flooded through Kensit as he felt Auralie's lips tightening around his stiff cock. Kensit began to shake. The exquisite sensation of her mouth on his prick was almost too much for him to bear. He could feel his sap rising. He wanted to come. But, expertly, Auralie gripped his penis at the base and held his orgasm back.

'Smack her bottom,' commanded Auralie. 'Smack it hard.'

Kensit brought his hand down on the soft flesh of the unknown girl.

'Again, and harder,' ordered Auralie.

Kensit did as he was told, his hand stinging from the contact.

'She belongs to a special sect,' explained Auralie. 'She must experience pleasure and pain. And pleasure with pain. And the pleasure of pain. She must live out all her secret desires. Feel her. Feel her pussy.' Auralie took the forefinger of Kensit's right hand, hooked it around her own then trailed it along the top of the girl's legs. 'She's wet. This bitch is very wet. Kensit, bend down and put your tongue just where I've got my finger.'

Kensit did as he was told and licked at the outer rim of the girl's labia. Auralie splayed her vulva lips wider so that Kensit's tongue could move easily and slurp in the girl's soft juiciness. There was a mirror opposite and from where he was kneeling Kensit could see Auralie's naked pussy as she bent forward. This gave an added impetus to his already stiff prick.

'Madame Olga wants you to screw her. Yes, your mistress has given permission,' Auralie reassured him, 'and this dirty bitch wants to be screwed. That's what she's been dreaming about, haven't you, slut?'

The girl's head gave a slight nod.

'You see, Kensit, that is why she kneels so still, so open and so wet. She wants to be taken by a stranger and you and I are going to give her her heart's desire. Take her. Take her fast.'

Kensit stood up and positioned himself. Auralie took hold of his cock and, leaning across the girl, whispered in his ear: 'Take her. Take her now, but use her arse. She's here to be improved. To know the pleasure of each orifice. Except her mouth. Today her mouth is gagged. Today she won't have that pleasure. Today she has to know the pleasure of a cock, a beautiful stiff cock in her anus. And, her anus needs to be stretched.'

The girl on the floor said nothing and remained utterly motionless. Auralie played with her wet vulva, taking some of its juices to lubricate her other opening. The girl's hips began to sway with a licentious roll. She was offering herself to Kensit. She was talking with her body, silently consenting to everything that was being done. Kensit came up between the girl's legs.

'This man is going to screw you now,' Auralie told the girl. 'He is going straight up into your pretty little arse.'

Kensit placed his hands on the girl's hips, aimed, and penetrated. With the force of his enthusiasm she shot forward. The habit covering the top half of the girl's body slipped awry and Kensit saw that not only was her mouth gagged but her hands were bound together and fastened to a long chain. She rolled back on to his penis, then jerked forward. He pulled her hips back hard, penetrating her deeper then smacked her plump, fleshy buttocks. Auralie smiled, lifted her own skirt and began to stroke herself with soft tantalising strokes. Kensit penetrated the girl again and again. And smacked her again and again. The girl rolled and heaved, and rocked and swayed, taking every last inch of him.

'Kensit, what are you doing?' roared Olga, walking into the study.

Kensit could not believe his ears. He had been seduced by the maid, taken by the niece, told that his employer wanted him to screw the chained girl and, thinking it was a condition of employment, was happily doing it. Yet now he was being asked what he was doing. Well, *screw her* because all he wanted to do now was come. He had been interrupted twice and this time he was going to manage it. He didn't care if he did lose his job. He wanted his orgasm.

'Screwing this young lady's arse, madam,' he replied boldly, continuing to jab, penetrate, hold and smack the girl, whose only sounds were muffled gasps of enjoyment.

Olga looked across at Auralie with a smile of amusement on her face.

'Impertinence,' said Olga. She walked over and ringed the base of his cock with her hand as Auralie juggled his balls.

'We wouldn't want to stop your pleasure . . .' said Auralie.

'Or ours,' added Olga. 'But . . .'

Kensit held his breath. Auralie was rolling his balls between her fingers and his mouth had gone completely dry.

'Don't look at her face,' Olga commanded, 'and when you've finished come into the drawing-room. We have a proposition to make to you.'

Auralie and Olga left the study, closing the door

behind them, leaving Kensit on his own with the chained girl

Kensit flicked his cock with his hands making certain it was as stiff as it could be, then he penetrated the girl's anus once more. He rode her hard, enjoying her delighted moans. He was going to come in a way he had never experienced before. He was excited beyond anything he had ever known. The gagged and chained girl with only her sex on show was opening, expanding under his thrusts. His whole body shuddered. He was reaching heights, pinnacles of desire and lust he had never known, never thought existed. And the covered girl continued to sway and moan, accepting, wanting, loving every jerk, jab and thrust he gave and her total compliance was taking him higher and higher, beyond himself into unknown territory.

Olga and Auralie went back to the drawing-room. The maid, having properly fulfilled her role in the charade of seducing Kensit, was now in the bedroom sorting out Olga's clothes and hanging them in the closet. The telephone rang. Nicole answered it. It was Sir Henry de Bouys's secretary. Nicole buzzed through on the intercom for Olga. Auralie listened to the conversation with a growing sense of disquiet. Annoyance was spreading across Olga's face and she was answering in monosyllables. There was a tone in Olga's voice that was odd. Auralie tried to analyse it. It was slightly put out, slightly petulant but conciliatory, not the usual Olga imperiousness.

'Yes, yes of course we understand,' Olga said. Then she turned to Auralie. 'Sir Henry's sorry, he

can't make London today. He's stayed in Rome.'
Olga turned back to the caller. 'Yes, of course. Of
course he must have a honeymoon, if only a short
one.'

'Honeymoon!' said Auralie. 'Who's he married?
Olga, who's he married?'

'And who is the fortunate lady?' Olga asked
airily. Her airiness changing dramatically with the
answer. 'Who?' she screeched. 'Who did you say?
Penelope Vladelsky!'

Auralie blanched at the news. Olga continued
talking. Auralie avoided her glance. She was dis-
tantly aware of Olga murmuring the usual congrat-
ulatory platitudes then ending the conversation,
but her mind had gone into a spin. Jeanine's
mother, her enemy, had married the man who
could save the company. Who could give them one
of the biggest furnishing contracts in the world. Her
father-in-law had married her aunt! God, how
incestuous! And she had been thinking of divorcing
Gerry. She could not do that now. She would have
to hold on to him with everything she had and with
everything she could do.

'Well . . . ?' said Olga.

'Disaster,' said Auralie.

'Disaster?' asked Olga.

'Yes, we'll never get the contract now,' said
Auralie. 'That woman hates me. Really hates me.'

'I've never understood why,' said Olga.

'You really don't know? Did Nin and Rea never
tell you?'

'No,' said Olga. 'Auralie, Sir Henry's coming to
London in four days and wants us to do the
presentation then. So, *chérie*, I think I should know

everything. Everything. But first tell me, your relationship with Jeanine, that's okay, isn't it?'

Olga watched Auralie's face fall.

'I see,' said Olga. 'Well, why does Penelope hate you?'

'She found me sucking Stefan's cock.'

'What!' shrieked Olga, then burst out laughing. 'Stefan! *Merde!* Her husband. Your uncle . . .'

'So's Petrov,' said Auralie.

'True, but Petrov is Petrov. Stefan. Holy bloody Stefan. But when, when did you do it?'

'It was on my eighteenth birthday. He was lying on his bed. He was naked but asleep and his prick looked so pretty I thought it would be nice to touch it. So I did. He didn't wake up, just sighed, so I touched it a bit more and it grew. Then I thought I wonder what it'd be like if I put it in my mouth. So I did. I was enjoying myself so much. He had a very big prick, you know. Well, I thought so at the time. Anyway I didn't hear Penelope come in.'

'What happened?'

'She screamed and threw me out of the house. That's when I came to stay with you. As you know, she said she'd never speak to me again, and she never has.'

'Umm, well I think we'd better discuss the whole thing with Petrov.'

'Petrov?'

'Yes. Perhaps he'll have some ideas. You see, *chérie*, it's quite simple. With the state of the market at the moment, without that contract as a company we are finished. We must have it. Now, of course, there is one simple way. We de-hire you as our designer.'

'What! You couldn't! You wouldn't.'

'*Chérie*, this is business. Business is a jungle. There are no friends or relatives in business, not if it means failure. But I don't want to do that. So, we go and see Petrov. Perhaps he'll have another, and better, idea.'

Olga rang the bell for Kensit who quickly appeared, naked and expectant in the doorway.

'All our plans have been changed,' Olga said, all thought of sex erased from her mind. Now there was only money and survival, and the change in her attitude showed in her voice. Kensit felt it keenly, stood to attention and almost saluted.

'Put your clothes on. You're driving us to my husband's house in the country,' Olga added.

Not one of the three spoke as they made their way down in the lift to the limousine parked outside. And the silence continued to reign until they were safely ensconced with Petrov, when all hell was let loose.

BLACK
lace

Published in April

GOTHIC BLUE
Portia Da Costa

A handsome young nobleman falls under the spell of a malevolent but irresistible sorceress. Two hundred years later, Belinda Seward also falls prey to incomprehensible and uncontrollable sexual forces. Stranded in a thunderstorm at a remote Gothic priory, she and her boyfriend are drawn into an enclosed world of luxurious decadence and sexual alchemy. And their host, a melancholic, lovelorn aristocrat, has plans for Belinda – plans which will take her into the realms of obsessive love and the erotic paranormal.

ISBN 0 352 33075 9

THE HOUSE OF GABRIEL
Rafaella

Journalist Jessica Martyn is researching a feature on lost treasures of erotic art for a glossy women's magazine. Her quest takes her to the elegant Jacobean mansion of the enigmatic Gabriel Martineaux, and she is gradually drawn into a sensual world of strange power games and costumed revelry. She also finds trouble, in the shape of her arch-rival Araminta Harvey.

ISBN 0 352 33063 5

Published in May

PANDORA'S BOX
ed. Kerri Sharp

This unique anthology of erotic writing by women brings together new material with extracts from the best-selling and most popular titles in the Black Lace series. *Pandora's Box* is a celebration of this revolutionary imprint which put women's erotic fiction in the media spotlight. The diversity of the material is a testament to the many facets of the female erotic imagination.

ISBN 0 352 33074 0

THE NINETY DAYS OF GENEVIEVE
Lucinda Carrington

When Genevieve Loften enters into a business deal with the arrogant and attractive James Sinclair, she doesn't expect a 90-day sex contract to be part of the bargain. As a career move, though, the pay-off promises to make it worth her while. Thrown into a world of sexual challenges, Genevieve learns how to balance a high-pressure career with the twilight world of fetishism and debauchery.

ISBN 0 352 33070 8

To be published in June

THE BIG CLASS
Angel Strand

1930s Europe. As Hitler and Mussolini are building their war machine, Cia – a young Anglo-Italian woman – is on her way back to England, leaving behind a complex web of sexual adventures. Her enemies are plotting revenge and deception and her Italian lover has disappeared – as has her collection of designer clothes. In England her friends are sailing their yachts and partying, but this facade hides tensions, rivalries and forbidden pleasures in which Cia becomes embroiled. It's only a matter of time before her two worlds collide – and everyone has to face up to their responsibilities.

ISBN 0 352 33076 7

THE BLACK ORCHID HOTEL
Roxanne Carr

Many contented female clients have passed through the Black Orchid Hotel, and, as joint owner of this luxurious pleasure palace, Maggie can have her every need satisfied at any time. But she has begun to tire of her sophisticated lovers, and is soon encouraging the attentions of the more rugged men in the area – including the local fire officer and a notorious biker. But she had better beware. There is one new friendship which may prove to be too hot to handle.

ISBN 0 352 33060 0

If you would like a complete list of plot summaries of Black Lace titles, please fill out the questionnaire overleaf or send a stamped addressed envelope to:-

Black Lace
332 Ladbroke Grove
London W10 5AH

BLACK
lace

WE NEED YOUR HELP ...
to plan the future of women's erotic fiction –

– and no stamp required!

Yours are the only opinions that matter.
Black Lace is the first series of books devoted to erotic fiction by women for women.
We intend to keep providing the best-written, sexiest books you can buy. And we'd appreciate your help and valued opinion of the books so far. Tell us what you want to read.

THE BLACK LACE QUESTIONNAIRE

SECTION ONE: ABOUT YOU

1.1 Sex (*we presume you are female, but so as not to discriminate*)
Are you?
Male ☐
Female ☐

1.2 Age
under 21 ☐ 21–30 ☐
31–40 ☐ 41–50 ☐
51–60 ☐ over 60 ☐

1.3 At what age did you leave full-time education?
still in education ☐ 16 or younger ☐
17–19 ☐ 20 or older ☐

1.4 Occupation _____

1.5 Annual household income
   under £10,000 ☐   £10–£20,000 ☐
   £20–£30,000 ☐   £30–£40,000 ☐
   over £40,000 ☐

1.6 We are perfectly happy for you to remain anonymous;
   but if you would like to receive information on other
   publications available, please insert your name and
   address

   _____
   _____
   _____
   _____

SECTION TWO: ABOUT BUYING BLACK LACE BOOKS

2.1 How did you acquire this copy of *Pandora's Box*?
   I bought it myself ☐   My partner bought it ☐
   I borrowed/found it ☐

2.2 How did you find out about Black Lace books?
   I saw them in a shop ☐
   I saw them advertised in a magazine ☐
   I saw the London Underground posters ☐
   I read about them in _____
   Other _____

2.3 Please tick the following statements you agree with:
   I would be less embarrassed about buying Black
   Lace books if the cover pictures were less explicit ☐
   I think that in general the pictures on Black
   Lace books are about right ☐
   I think Black Lace cover pictures should be as
   explicit as possible ☐

2.4 Would you read a Black Lace book in a public place – on
   a train for instance?
   Yes ☐   No ☐

SECTION THREE: ABOUT THIS BLACK LACE BOOK

3.1 Do you think the sex content in this book is:
    Too much   ☐   About right   ☐
    Not enough   ☐

3.2 Do you think the writing style in this book is:
    Too unreal/escapist ☐   About right   ☐
    Too down to earth   ☐

3.3 Do you think the story in this book is:
    Too complicated   ☐   About right   ☐
    Too boring/simple   ☐

3.4 Do you think the cover of this book is:
    Too explicit   ☐   About right   ☐
    Not explicit enough ☐

Here's a space for any other comments:

SECTION FOUR: ABOUT OTHER BLACK LACE BOOKS

4.1 How many Black Lace books have you read?   ☐

4.2 If more than one, which one did you prefer?

4.3 Why?

SECTION FIVE: ABOUT YOUR IDEAL EROTIC NOVEL

We want to publish the books you want to read – so this is your chance to tell us exactly what your ideal erotic novel would be like.

5.1 Using a scale of 1 to 5 (1 = no interest at all, 5 = your ideal), please rate the following possible settings for an erotic novel:

Medieval/barbarian/sword 'n' sorcery ☐
Renaissance/Elizabethan/Restoration ☐
Victorian/Edwardian ☐
1920s & 1930s – the Jazz Age ☐
Present day ☐
Future/Science Fiction ☐

5.2 Using the same scale of 1 to 5, please rate the following themes you may find in an erotic novel:

Submissive male/dominant female ☐
Submissive female/dominant male ☐
Lesbianism ☐
Bondage/fetishism ☐
Romantic love ☐
Experimental sex e.g. anal/watersports/sex toys ☐
Gay male sex ☐
Group sex ☐

Using the same scale of 1 to 5, please rate the following styles in which an erotic novel could be written:

Realistic, down to earth, set in real life ☐
Escapist fantasy, but just about believable ☐
Completely unreal, impressionistic, dreamlike ☐

5.3 Would you prefer your ideal erotic novel to be written from the viewpoint of the main male characters or the main female characters?

Male ☐ Female ☐
Both ☐

5.4 What would your ideal Black Lace heroine be like? Tick as many as you like:

Dominant	☐	Glamorous	☐
Extroverted	☐	Contemporary	☐
Independent	☐	Bisexual	☐
Adventurous	☐	Naive	☐
Intellectual	☐	Introverted	☐
Professional	☐	Kinky	☐
Submissive	☐	Anything else?	☐
Ordinary	☐		

_____

5.5 What would your ideal male lead character be like? Again, tick as many as you like:

Rugged	☐		
Athletic	☐	Caring	☐
Sophisticated	☐	Cruel	☐
Retiring	☐	Debonair	☐
Outdoor-type	☐	Naive	☐
Executive-type	☐	Intellectual	☐
Ordinary	☐	Professional	☐
Kinky	☐	Romantic	☐
Hunky	☐		
Sexually dominant	☐	Anything else?	☐
Sexually submissive	☐		

_____

5.6 Is there one particular setting or subject matter that your ideal erotic novel would contain?

_____

SECTION SIX: LAST WORDS

6.1 What do you like best about Black Lace books?

_____

6.2 What do you most dislike about Black Lace books?

_____

6.3 In what way, if any, would you like to change Black Lace covers?

_____

6.4   Here's a space for any other comments:

_____

_____

_____

_____

_____

Thank you for completing this questionnaire. Now tear it out of the book – carefully! – put it in an envelope and send it to:

Black Lace
FREEPOST
London
W10 5BR

No stamp is required if you are resident in the U.K.